BLOOD ON CELLULOID

Other Books by B. L. Morgan

Blood and Rain
Blood for the Masses
Night Knuckles

BLOOD ON CELLULOID

B. L. MORGAN

SPEAKING VOLUMES, LLC

NAPLES, FLORIDA

2011

BLOOD ON CELLULOID

ISBN 978-1-61232-022-9

Library of Congress Control Number: 2010942890

BOOK ONE

PART I

A STEP INTO THE HOUSE OF PAIN

PROLOGUE

December
9:00 A.M

White scratched at my eyes and dug a hole all the way to the back of my brain, creating an ache that I had a feeling would never go away. All the walls inside the East St. Louis Morgue were painted a harsh white. Bright neon flared from everywhere. The smell of formaldehyde burned my nostrils.

Everything about this place told me to run and not look back and do not, DO NOT, take a look under the sheet that lay spread over the body in the center of the room.

The harsh white light speared my brain. I'd never felt this bad when I was on a hangover from my worst drinking binge. Then, I didn't care. The pain was only my body doing a slow slide toward death.

Now, I hadn't touched a drink for at least six months and was cold sober.

I froze just inside the door. I didn't know I had. Everything just shut down, my mind, my body. Maybe my unconsciousness was saying to the rest of me, *Stand here long enough and you'll wake up. It'll be just one more nightmare and she'll be OK.*

East St. Louis Police Detective Joe Briggs touched me on the elbow. "I know this is gonna be hard," he said. "But you gotta do it."

I moved forward. Everything seemed out of kilter. The floor seemed to be further away than it should be.

I walked to the autopsy table.

The man standing beside the table was thin and nervous. A name tag read, Charles. He looked like he wanted to be anywhere other than where he was at that moment.

I wanted the same thing.

I reached out and touched the sheet and took it in my hand. I took a deep breath. My hand fell to my side as though it wasn't a part of me.

The thin nervous man stepped up to the opposite side of the table. "I'm sorry," he said. "I should do this."

He pulled the sheet down.

The perfect features of my woman were revealed by the descending cloth.

Sherry St. Claire, the woman who saved me from myself was dead. She gave me a reason to stay straight and not fill my body full of poison.

Now she was dead.

Joe Briggs asked, "Is that her?"

"You know it is," I answered. A buzzing filled my ears.

I'd seen death before. I'd caused more than my share of people to be put in the ground. It never bothered me to look closely at a corpse before but this time it was different. This was not just some cold slab of meat.

This was the woman I loved.

Her face was a grimace of pain.

I reached out and pulled the sheet down and off her naked body.

"Wait," the thin nervous man named Charles said. "You're only here to identify her. You can't do that."

The look I gave Charles made him take two quick steps backward. The look told him if he would have been within arm's reach I would have knocked his teeth out.

Sherry had been a beautiful woman, slim and attractive with all the right curves in all the right places. She was a mix of Asian and Caucasian parents. I always thought she got the best from both races.

Now, both her nipples had been torn off. It looked like something like pliers had been used to rip them loose. Huge purple bruises and small cuts were up and down the sides of her arms, legs and torso. Oddly, her face had remained untouched.

Her throat was slashed.

Sherry St. Claire had been beaten and tortured, then murdered.

Joe Briggs grabbed me from behind by the arms and hauled me backward. He was a big black bear of a man. I couldn't have stopped him if I'd wanted to. I didn't try to stop him.

I'd seen enough.

One glance showed me everything I needed to know. My woman had died after suffering extended extreme pain.

Joe pulled me to the door and we ascended the stairs in silence.

A cold rage was filling me.

Sherry was dead!

I would never hold her in my arms again and kiss her soft lips. I would never laugh with her again.

Sherry was dead and it was my fault.

Outside the East St. Louis Morgue Joe Briggs broke the silence.

"You got yourself together real good John. I didn't think you could. But you did. I'll see to this case myself. I liked Sherry. Don't do anything crazy."

"You know me better than that," I told him and the look I gave Joe let him know that I'd make somebody pay for this.

CHAPTER 1

Where do you go when there's no where you want to go?

Who do you speak with when the only person you want to talk to is dead?

*   *   *

I started by going to the upscale gentleman's club that Sherry owned named Patty's Kitten House, and telling the bartender to announce that the place was closed until tomorrow and everyone had to leave.

Officially I was no more than Sherry's bodyguard and a bouncer at the club but everyone knew me and Sherry were together so less than ten minutes later the customers were gone, the doors were locked and the dancers, the bouncers, the bartender and the parking lot attendants were clustered around me wanting to know what was up.

I didn't mince any words. There was no sense in doing that.

"I just got back from the morgue," I told them. "I identified Sherry's body."

There was a stunned silence. A few of the dancers held each other and wept in each others arms. Somebody said, "No!"

Ron Martin, a large blond haired country boy of a man who was an ex-linebacker for the St. Louis Cardinals, was standing beside me.

"You know how to run this place?" I asked him.

"Yeah, I can do that," he answered.

"Good," I told him. "You're in charge until told otherwise."

I asked the room, "Does anyone here know how to arrange for a funeral?"

One of the parking lot attendants, a small black guy named Paul Harris, said he'd taken care of the arrangements when his grandfather passed away.

I asked him if he would arrange Sherry's funeral. He said he would.

"Ron, give him what money he needs," I said. "Take it from the company bank account."

Ron nodded.

I said to Paul, "Don't spare any expenses. Do something nice for her."

"I will Mr. Dark," he answered.

"Write yourself a check for whatever you figure your time is worth," I told him.

"You don't have to do that," Paul said. "I don't want nothing for doing this."

"I know," I told him. "Pay yourself something anyway."

CHAPTER 2

East St. Louis in December is bleak. Stark cold sinks through your clothes, and bitter winds drive the icy feeling all the way down and into your bones.

I drove to the East St. Louis Police Department. My car now was a black Porsche, a gift from Sherry. My ancient Olds Delta 88 was parked in the far corner of the parking lot of Patty's Kitten House. It was a beat up old rod with a reliable motor that had seen better days. I'm not sure why I kept the thing.

The day Sherry gave me the Porsche I told her, "Hey babe, if I'd have known slinging my meat would get me this kind of stuff I'd have went into that business a long time ago."

She laughed and punched me in the stomach.

"You're good," Sherry said. "But no one's that good."

We kissed then and when we went to bed that night I tried to prove to her that I was that good.

Thinking about that made me feel like crying.

*   *   *

The East St. Louis Police Department was, as usual, a zoo. Prostitutes were arguing with cops that their constitutional right to give blow jobs in alleys was being violated. Pimps were arguing that their right to sell women's asses on the street was being denied. Drug dealers argued that denying them the freedom of choice to sell poison to children was immoral. Thieves were arguing that in a free market economy it was wrong to deny them access to the wealth and goods that others had earned.

Everybody was arguing about something.

I couldn't be a cop. Somebody starts arguing with me about something and I'd just shoot the mother-fucker in the head and say, "I won that argument, idiot!"

The Desk Sergeant was arguing with some big fat ugly black broad about her crack-head sneak-thief son being locked up for purse snatching.

"I'm going to see Joe Briggs," I shouted at him loud enough to drown out the woman's complaints for a moment.

He made a motion with his head that said, "Go ahead," and continued his argument.

After making my way through a jungle of desks and arguing idiots I arrived at Joe Briggs' desk.

An argument was going on there too.

While standing and waiting, I got the gist of it.

A burglar, a young black guy with a pockmarked face, was sitting at Joe's desk. He was being released on a technicality and he wanted his burglary tools back. He actually said, "Those are the tools of my trade and you are denying me the right to earn a living."

I'd heard enough already. My patience was in short supply and I don't have much to begin with.

I leaned my face down into the black guy's face, close enough to think, *Fuck, this guy stinks* and said, "Get your ass out of that goddamned chair and get the fuck out of here!"

"You can't talk to me like that," he said. "Not in a police department. You cops can't do that shit!"

"I'm not a fucking cop," I told him and picked him up by his collar and dropped him onto the floor.

The man looked at Briggs.

"You best leave," Briggs told him. "I can only arrest John after he breaks your neck."

The guy scrambled to his feet and shuffled toward the door shouting at us, "I'm gonna file charges!"

"Good," I shouted back. I sat down in the vacated chair.

Joe looked at me over the top of his desk, over the top of a tall stack of unlooked-at case files.

"I know why you're here," Joe said. "I already told you I'll see to Sherry's case personally. I'm not gonna give you any information."

"You'll see to her case like maybe after you take care of those, right?" I pointed at the stack. "I'm going to find out who killed Sherry whether you want to help or not!"

"Look John, I know how you feel..."

"No you fucking don't!" I shouted at him and jumped to my feet. I leaned on the desk toward Joe.

"Did you just see your wife dead and fucking ripped apart by some sack of shit that needs to be dead? Did you?"

"Look John," Joe started.

I cut him off. "Look my ass," I told him. "I'll tell you how I feel." I locked eyes with Joe. "I don't feel anything right now. I'm a dead man. I'm dead inside. I don't give a fuck!"

I sat back down.

Between us, there was a silence thick enough to cut with a knife. In the rest of the room everything continued, in the rest of the world the clock ticked and life went on, but here we were frozen.

Time stopped.

I broke the silence with, "I just want to know where she was found. I'll find out eventually anyway and if I have to hurt some of your precious citizens to do that, you know I will."

Joe thought for a moment then said, "I'll make a bargain with you. You find out anything, you share it with me and we'll take these guys down together, deal?"

"Deal," I answered. I'd have told him anything to find out what I wanted to know and Joe knew that.

"Sherry was found in the vacant lot at State Street and Fifth Avenue at twelve-fifteen last night. There were no clues. The usual trash was blowing around but nothing out of the ordinary. The ground was frozen so there were no footprints left behind. That's it, nothing else to tell you."

"Why do you think two were involved?" I asked Joe.

He started at the question.

"You let that slip," I told him.

"It's just a hunch," Joe answered. "Sherry was a healthy woman with a little martial arts in her background. She was always aware of her surroundings. She wouldn't have gone without a fight. Whoever took Sherry did it fast and without much of a struggle. I'm guessing it had to be at least two men."

I stood up and shook hands with Joe.

"You find out who they are," he said. "You bring them to me."

"Do you think I'm really going to do that?" I asked.

"No," he answered.

"Good, then we understand each other. You did your job telling me to follow the law. I'll do what I have to do," I told him. "I'll let you know where their bodies are when I'm done."

CHAPTER 3

There wasn't shit out at State Street and Fifth Avenue, not a goddamn thing. The vacant lot covered almost a half block area. It probably measured around a half-acre of ground.

No fence separated the vacant lot from anything else, but seeing where the boundaries were set up wasn't a problem. Around the lot were vacant, old, weathered, rotting houses. In its best days this area never had very many people live out here and I doubt this area ever had any best days.

About a half block away from the lot was a combination all night liquor store and tobacconist shop. The guy who ran that place probably made the majority of his business after the bars closed and he likely made it selling drugs. Out here, nobody would give a shit anyway.

A little farther away than that was an adult bookstore and triple x video arcade. There were a few cars parked in front of that place. The guys inside were probably in the booths beating their meat to the images of orgasmic females getting their brains fucked out. Or there were faggots in the booths swallowing each other's tube steak.

There was nothing else around except for boarded up businesses and emptiness. There weren't even any bums around here laying between the buildings. I guess they stay in the areas where they can at least get hold of some food.

Out here there wasn't shit to eat.

I parked the Porsche next to the curb at the vacant lot, got out and walked out onto the hard frozen earth. In the center of the lot a large square had been marked off with stakes and yellow crime scene tape.

It was a barren spot.

Dead weeds lay dried out and crumpled over. Paper things, candy wrappers, liquor store receipts blew into and out of the square.

Joe was right. There was nothing here.

I looked at the ground, the cold hard-packed frozen dead earth. This is the place where someone had dumped my woman's body.

Sherry was a lady who was accustomed to the finest silk sheets. She earned the money to live well and believed in enjoying it.

Someone threw her onto harsh dirt.

I was going to find out who that was and teach them the meaning of harsh.

*   *   *

I went in the liquor and tobacco store and went up to the counter. A white guy with stringy long brown hair sat in a folding chair reading a porno magazine behind the counter.

He looked at me when I walked up to him.

"I need to ask you about last night," I told him.

"Police already been all over me about that," he answered.

"Yeah, but I'm here now," I told him.

"Fuck it," he said. "Same as I told them, I didn't see shit. I was here all night. Look at the door you came in," he pointed to the front of the store.

Boxes of different kinds of whiskeys and wines and beers were stacked at least chest high in front of the plate glass window. A big life-size Tecate advertisement, with a sweet Mexican broad looking like she was going to deep throat a long neck bottle, was between the counter and the glass door.

"I was right here all night," he said. "Anything that happened outside, I wouldn't have been able to have seen it."

I could see what he meant. He probably kept the place like this to stop anybody from seeing the deals he did inside.

I left him my name and number and headed over to the porno shop.

*   *   *

On a day that seemed like it would never end, evening was crawling over the land in shades of deepening gray.

The outside of Ray's Triple X Gallery was brightly lit with neon lights. The plate glass window was painted white from the inside. An iron mesh grill sealed off the door from the outside world.

A sign was taped to the door from inside the wire mesh that read, "No one under the age of 21 allowed on premises!"

I entered the door and a hanging cow bell clunked behind me. Two guys were browsing through the fuck magazines looking so closely at the pictures it seemed like they wanted to absorb the images through their skin.

The place inside was brightly lit and had a pungent odor to it. I was hoping I wasn't smelling the buckets of cum that was left on the floor in the booths in the back. Although that idea made me want to gag, that's probably what it was.

Weird techno rock was playing in the background. I think it was some shit they call Industrial, lots of shrieks and machine noises backed up by a synthesized drum beat. Just barely heard drifting in from the back rooms where they had the beaters booths was the sound of moans and heavy breathing from the porno films being played, paid for by the quarter.

I walked directly to the counter. A guy with three rings through his lip, a tattooed shaved head and mirrored sunglasses went out of his way to ignore me. He turned his back and started running his fingers over rows of boxes of VHS tapes and old super 8 films of all manner of fuck films like he was looking for something. Above the movies was a display showing camcorders and Super 8 and 8 Millimeter movie cameras.

"Hey," I said to him. "I need to talk to you about last night."

"I've said all I'm going say to you pigs," he answered and kept right on ignoring me.

That was the second time today someone had mistaken me for being a cop. I didn't know if I liked that or not.

"This is a personal inquiry," I told him.

He snorted a laugh. "Then get the fuck out of my place," he said. "You're bad for business."

I took a business card that was on his counter, wrote my name and number on the back of it, and laid it on the counter at the same time as saying, "This'll only take a minute."

"I told you to get the fuck out of my place," he said and snatched the card up and backhand threw it at me.

The card bounced off my forehead.

I grabbed his hand out of the air with my left hand, twisted it and snapped a hard right jab into his teeth, then jerked him over the counter and threw him to the floor.

He bounced off a display of dildos and I got on top of him straddling him, pinning his arms to the tile with my knees.

"Now you want to talk to me shit-head?" I shouted at him.

"Fuck you!" He shouted back. "The bitch should have stayed home. She fucked around with the wrong people and got fucked up!"

I leaned into his face. "Who was it?" I yelled.

"I don't fucking know. I didn't see shit," he said.

I slammed a good straight right down into his face that made his head bounce off the tile and his eyes rolled around in his head. I did that just because it felt good.

The card I wrote my name and number on was lying on the floor beside his head. I picked it up and shoved it into his open mouth.

"You start remembering something, you call me. I find out you know something and don't tell me I'll come back and hurt you so bad you'll wish you were fucking dead."

I got up off him and the guys at the magazines were staring at me.

"Unless you want a piece of this," I told them. "Keep your face in that fucking book and forget that I was here."

Their eyes snapped back to the pictures on the paper.

I left.

CHAPTER 4

I probably should not have slapped that idiot around but so fucking what. He needed a good ass-whipping and I needed to whip somebody's ass. So we both came out even.

I drove back toward downtown East St. Louis, not even sure of where I wanted to go. I drove out of habit. My hand drifted to the radio. I switched it on, also out of habit.

Music came out and blared at me.

Driving along through the outskirts of town I switched the radio through all kinds of stations.

Nothing sounded good.

Music would never sound the same.

It was cold as hell outside but I didn't turn on the heater in the Porsche. I didn't want to feel warm.

I drove around thinking, trying to figure out what to do next and coming up with nothing.

I drove around thinking, trying to not feel anything.

I drifted past downtown, past Johnny's Bar and Grill and considered going inside and telling my best friend what happened but what the hell good would that do?

What was I supposed to do, go inside and have him and Jeanette give me hugs and pat me on the back and tell me that everything is going to be OK.

Fuck that!

Nothing is ever going back to being just fine and dandy. Nothing is ever going to be OK ever again.

Yesterday was our day off from the club. Around noon Sherry told me she had an errand to run and she'd be back in about an hour.

I gave her a kiss and lay around and watched TV.

She never came home.

I waited four hours then called Patty's Kitten House to see if she stopped by there. No one had seen or heard from her.

I waited another few hours then I called the police to check to see if there had been any bad car wrecks: Nothing. They took my name and number and said you have to wait at least seventy-two hours before you can file a missing persons report.

I wanted to go look for her but where the hell do you even start? Sherry's club was her life. Before I came along she didn't even take days off from work. She ran that place seven days a week. If Sherry had any family she never talked about them except when she told me her mother and father's names and that was it.

She had no outside interests that I knew about. Sherry was driven to make Patty's Kitten House a success. It was what she did. It was who she was.

During the next ten hours everything possible ran through my head. Did Sherry have a guy on the side? What did she have going on that I didn't know about after a year with this woman?

Tom, my big calico cat walked around the apartment meowing like he knew something was wrong.

I watched TV although I didn't really see the pictures. I drifted off to sleep on the couch somewhere around four or five in the morning.

At eight-thirty a knock came on the door.

Joe Briggs was standing there. That's when the real pain started.

*   *   *

It was early in the evening, early in December but the sky was already black as coal. It was too early to go home to an empty apartment but where the hell was I supposed to go?

I didn't even drink anymore so going and getting wasted was out of the question, even if it did seem like a good idea.

People were starting to put out the Christmas lights. This was the season for families to get closer. Family was the last thing I wanted to be thinking about.

Sherry was the only family that I had.

She was gone.

The good thing about not drinking anymore and killing hundreds of brain cells every night is that after a while I started being able to think clear again. I wasn't just reacting to life going on around me.

The bad thing about not drinking anymore is that I have no choice but to think. I couldn't stop myself.

As I drove around in circles in the city of St. Louis I thought too much.

There was no doubt in my mind that whoever killed Sherry had done it to get to me. Sherry had never done anything to anybody to make someone hate her so much that they'd torture her to death.

I had done a lot of things that would make people want to come after me, so I'd have to go and start shaking the trees in my old neighborhood and see what nuts fell to the ground.

The blinking Christmas lights twinkling in the store windows of downtown St. Louis were depressing so I went home.

The doorman at the Blaine Building knew me. He was reading a magazine that he barely looked up from and waved me past.

That was good.

I didn't want to talk to him or anybody else.

I took the elevator to our apartment and went in. Tom was on the couch waiting for me. I sat down beside him and looked around the place.

The entire apartment was decorated in Art Deco black and white. The place was immaculate. It was stylish and classy just like the lady that picked out all the furniture.

I sat down beside Tom and patted him on the head.

He sat beside me and stared into my eyes unblinking. He hardly ever did that.

"Looks like it's back to you and me, Bud." I told him and the words caught in my throat.

Later on that night, much later, I climbed into bed. I closed my eyes and the scent of Sherry was still on her pillow and inside the sheets.

I closed my eyes and willed myself to remember the silky feel of her black hair, the softness of her lips and the warmth of her skin. I willed myself to remember the sound of her sighs as we made love.

I made myself relive touching Sherry and every time I could almost sink deep enough into my memory, deep enough back into my mind to almost reach out and take her in my arms I would start to hear her scream.

She wouldn't stop until I opened my eyes and left the dream I'd sunk into.

I wanted to touch the memory of Sherry but I couldn't stop the screaming.

I couldn't stop hearing her scream!

CHAPTER 5

Piano music seemed to be coming from everywhere. My head was buzzing as I opened my eyes. My eyes felt puffy and scratchy like dirt had been ground into them.

The piano music went on.

The ghost of Beethoven was taking revenge for...hell, I don't know what he was taking revenge for. I never did anything to him. The piano music sounded tinny and slightly out of tune. I recognized the tune. It was something that Sherry really liked.

I could put up with it but it really wasn't my thing. My kind of music was Rush, Nazareth, Led Zeppelin or The Rolling Stones, long hair music of another sort.

It was the cell phone ringing.

I fell out of bed and grabbed it off the dresser.

"What's up?" I asked.

"It's Paul Harris at Patty's," the voice on the other end said. "I was making Sherry's arrangements and wanted to do it right so I figured I'd notify her relatives for you. You got enough on your mind right now and..."

"You don't have to explain," I told him. "I appreciate you thinking of it."

"Well, I figured she'd have an address book in her office but I can't find anything except names and numbers of business contacts. If you can find her address book there I'll call whoever you want and let them know about what happened."

"I'll look for it and give you a call back when I got some names and numbers for you."

I hung up and put Sherry's cell phone in my jacket pocket.

I stumbled around the apartment for a while.

Sherry got me used to drinking coffee in the mornings. Hell, she got me used to getting up in the mornings. So I went to the coffee maker.

I only drink this shit. I'd never made any before. I didn't have a clue as to how to make coffee. *What the fuck*, I thought. *It can't be that goddamned hard.*

After grabbing the can of coffee out of the cabinet I spooned a bunch of it, I don't have a clue how much, into this black plastic funnel thing that slides in over the top of the pot.

Then I filled the coffee maker with six cups of water and flipped on the switch and let it do its thing.

In the bathroom I brushed my teeth and looked in the mirror. I looked like hell. Guess a few days with only a few hours' sleep will do that to you.

After the three S's: a shower, a shit and a shave, I went back into the kitchen to get my cup of coffee.

I got a cup, poured it without looking and took a big gulp.

Slimy acrid tasting gravel was in my mouth.

I spit the stuff into the sink and looked at my cup. The black coffee was swimming in grounds.

I poured the whole fucking thing down the drain and got dressed and went to McDonalds for breakfast.

* * *

Back at the apartment I started looking through the drawers of Sherry's dresser.

Nothing is quite as enlightening as realizing that you never really knew the woman you loved and the reason you never knew her was because you never took the time to find out.

I went through Sherry's things and found out very little. What little information I did find out was so vague that it almost seemed like Sherry was hiding the information even from herself.

I had never asked Sherry about her family. Basically, I didn't care. What did it matter to me who her mother and father and aunts and uncles were? I wasn't fucking them.

As I moved around the clothing and personal items in Sherry's dresser drawers looking for something that might have phone numbers or addresses in it I realized that my not taking interest in Sherry's past was less respect for privacy than it was just laziness.

Getting close to Sherry was good for me. I hadn't cared if I was good for her.

In the second drawer I was going through, the drawer where Sherry kept her silk panties and lacy bras, I found an old battered black address book.

There weren't too many names inside.

Most of the names were of people I recognized from the club.

One stood out: Sister Mary Sheridon. Her address was The St. Wisdom Orphanage, 2020 Udon Way, Tehan Setar. There was a telephone number.

I put the address book in my pocket.

CHAPTER 6

I drove over to Patty's Kitten House and was met by a circus going on at the front door. There were three white news vans with their stations' call letters on the side: KXOK, KTVI and KDNL were blocking the entrance to the club.

Three news reporters with their camera crews were harassing everyone coming and going on the street. No one could get in or out of Patty's Kitten House without having a microphone shoved on their face.

Ron Martin was waving his arms and shouting at the reporters. Everyone that seemed to be driving up to the club would just slow down then drive on past.

After pulling around and parking in our private parking lot I went to the front entrance.

"What the hell's going on here?" I asked Ron and immediately had three microphones shoved in my face.

"Get those the fuck away from me!" I shouted at the three reporters. Two of them were damn good looking women. The other one was a guy who looked like he spent too much time gazing with affection at his own reflection in the mirror.

Ron said, "These idiots won't leave. Nobody's going to come in with them here. The customers inside can't leave either. Hell, they're like prisoners."

I turned my attention back to the three reporters.

"Get your goddamned equipment off my sidewalk!" I yelled at them.

They didn't back off one bit. They were like sharks circling their prey.

The male reporter said, "Buddy, just informing you that this sidewalk is city property and we can be here just as long as we want to be, and there's nothing you can do about it."

The two women reporters nodded their heads in agreement just like the bobble-head figurines that they were.

I turned to walk into the club and Mr. My-Teeth-Are-So-Bright-I-Must-Brush-Them-With-Cum grabbed my left arm. "Look," he said. "Give us our story and we'll leave. Don't, we'll be here forever."

I looked at the hand still clutching my arm. "Just informing you," I told him. "The instant you touched me you committed assault. I'm defending myself."

I snapped out a good hard straight overhand right to the guy's nose and felt a satisfying crunch when it landed.

I broke that mother-fucker's nose with the first shot and it felt good!

He staggered back and fell to his ass on the pavement.

The two women reporter's mouths were froze open in surprise. One of them had bleached blond hair and thick ruby red lips.

I don't know what possessed me, guess it was those lips. I asked big lips, "You want an interview?"

"Y-yeah, of course," she said.

"Then drop on your knees and swallow my sausage and make me sing Rudolf the Red Nosed Reindeer."

Her eyes widened so much I thought they would fall out of her head. One of the cameramen laughed.

"I didn't think so! That's the only fucking way you're getting an interview from me!"

I waved Ron with me and we both went inside Patty's Kitten House and locked the door behind us.

*   *   *

Our Disc Jockey was a dedicated guy. He was still spinning his records even though there were only two customers in the place and one dancer was entertaining them.

I told Ron what to do and asked where Paul Harris was. Ron told me that Paul was in Sherry's office. I went back there.

As I was heading to Sherry's office the music stopped and the Disc Jockey's voice came over the PA. "Sorry guys," the DJ said. "We're closing down until we can get those reporters out of our hair. Leave your name with our lovely hostess at the front door and next time you come in there will be no cover charge."

In Sherry's office Paul Harris had a list he'd compiled of possible people to call. All of them were business contacts. I told him to call all of them.

We sat down and added the names from Sherry's address book that weren't already on the list. I added the names of Johnny Davis and his grandmother Jeanette to the list.

The list of people to notify of Sherry's death was very short and I couldn't help but ask myself, *where the hell was her family*.

Just before I left, Paul Harris handed me a box that contained Sherry's bank books and cancelled checks. I'd go through those when I got back home.

CHAPTER 7

News travels fast, especially bad news.

It took about an hour to get everybody out of Patty's Kitten House and get the place closed down and locked up.

I thought about going around and questioning my old contacts in the drug dealing trade to see if there was anybody who still had a serious grudge against me, but when I ran the list through my head I realized almost all those guys were dead, and the ones that weren't pushing up daisies were now crack heads. There's no way they would have the brains, the muscle, or the money to arrange for a murder like Sherry's had been.

Those guys could maybe sneak up behind someone with a rock and bash their brains in but kidnapping and torture were way outside their league.

I looked at the box of financial records sitting on the rider's seat of my Porsche and decided to head back to our apartment.

*   *   *

The circus was in town and it was at my front door.

The same three news crews that were at Patty's Kitten House were outside the front doors of The Blaine Building. The landlord/real estate manager of the complex was being interviewed.

This time the news crews were backed up by two police cars and the four cops that came with them. One of the cops was a guy who didn't like me one bit, Sergeant O'Malley. O'Malley was a big ugly Irish cop who was trying hard to become the poster boy for The Police Brutality is Fun Club.

If he was here, this was not good for me.

I parked and went to go in through the front doors. With the tight security they had in this place, there was no back entrance.

"Hold it right there!" O'Malley told me doing the raised palm traffic cop halt sign. O'Malley was his same old ugly self, except today maybe a little uglier. He was wearing a good long bloody scratch mark across his right cheek. "This is to inform you you've been ordered to quit the premises."

I looked over at Robert Cummings the landlord.

"What Officer O'Malley said is correct," Cummings spoke. "You have never been on Miss. St. Claire's lease and pursuant to part five, paragraph two, pertaining to undesirables, you are hereby evicted immediately. We used my passkey to gather your things."

He pointed at two suitcases and a cat carrier that Tom was inside. Tom looked really pissed off. He hissed whenever anyone moved or spoke, which was a lot of hissing.

O'Malley stepped close to my ear. He had his hand on his nightstick. "I knew I'd get you," he whispered. "I waited and I got you!"

He was clutching his nightstick like he wanted me to make a move. The three other cops had their sticks in their hands, slapping their palms with them. They wanted to be raising some knots but couldn't make the first move, not when the cameras were recording every second of what went on here.

"This is your day," I told O'Malley. "Enjoy it while you can."

I loaded my two suitcases into the trunk of my Porsche, then put the box of financial records on the floorboard, and loaded Tom in his carrier onto the rider seat.

Tom looked at me through the bars of his cage.

"Well at least you got a good shot in on O'Malley," I told him. "But why the hell did you have to miss his eye?"

His meow sounded like, "Sorry."

PART II

WELCOME BACK TO THE JUNGLE

CHAPTER 8

I drove away from The Blaine Building feeling not exactly pissed off but not exactly happy either. I wanted to bash O'Malley upside the head but I didn't need an excuse for that. He was just one of those guys I wanted to kick the shit out of.

The first order of business was finding a place to sleep tonight. I doubt the homeless shelters were going to let me in when I come driving up in my Porsche. So I drove to my old apartment building in good old scenic downtown East St. Louis.

The place was the same as when I'd left. It wouldn't change a bit until it collapsed completely into a pile of bricks and plaster and cockroaches. Maybe a few more of the windows were boarded up but that was about all that was different.

I went in the door and passed a hand written cardboard sign that read, Landlord Apt 312.

I climbed the stairs to the third floor having to step over two drunks on the stairway that were laying in their own vomit.

There was a freight elevator but the landlord kept it locked with a heavy disc lock that only he had the key to. I didn't blame him for keeping it locked up for his own use either. Around here, these boys will tear up anything. If he didn't keep it locked it'd be tore up in less than a week.

Rodney Fuller was the landlord. I knocked on his door and heard a muted, "Just a minute, hold on."

Then from the other side of the door and louder, "Who the fuck is it?"

"It's John Dark," I said. "Remember me?"

The door swung open.

"Come on in," Rodney answered and wheeled himself back away from the door. Rodney Fuller was a big black man who lost his legs in the Viet Nam War. He didn't cry about how unfair life was and stay drunk and drugged up until the day he died. Instead he took advantage of every government program he could get his hands on. After a lot of wheeling and dealing through the years Rodney owned this building and three others just like it.

The basic conveniences of hot and cold water, electricity, and heat were always in good working order in Rodney's buildings. They weren't luxurious but Rodney provided a low cost roof over your head.

Right now, that's what I needed.

"How you been, John?" He asked and we shook hands. "You're kind of famous today."

"You've been watching the news then." I sat down on a couch in front of a large screen color TV tuned to CNN.

"Always," he said. "Got to know what's going on in the world to get anywhere in the world. After your guest appearance on the morning news I figure you need a place to stay."

"You could say that," I answered.

"Shit," Rodney said. "Boy they bent you over and rammed you in the morning news. Sorry to hear about what happened to your lady."

"Not half as sorry as I am," I said.

"I bet. You know, they were saying you have a connection to your girl's murder."

"No, I didn't hear them say that. It's probably better that I didn't. I'd be in jail right now if I had. I ain't been watching the news," I told Rodney. "I've been living it."

"I heard that," he said. "Oh man! I like that shot you gave that pretty boy reporter. You want I can show it to you in slow-mo. I recorded that motherfucker. Camera had a good angle. Blood and snot flew out of both sides of his nose."

"Maybe later," I told him.

"You want your old place back?"

"You mean you ain't rented it in the year I've been gone?"

"I held it just in case you came back," he said. "Shit man, ain't nobody moving into East St. Louis, people trying to get out!"

"Yeah, I'll take it back. Is all the furniture still there?"

"Fuck, wasn't shit there worth stealing. People don't steal shit ain't worth carrying down the stairs. Rent's two-fifty, bro."

I grimaced. I had around two hundred in my pocket and only around a thousand in the bank. I knew I'd probably need the thousand to find Sherry's killer.

"I'm a little strapped at the moment," I told Rodney.

"Not a problem," he answered. "Just call me Mother-fucking-Father Christmas this year. Remember the deal we used to have where you evict who I need gone and you get rent credit?"

"Yeah, I remember."

"OK, I got these fucking winos that were sleeping in the halls. I'd get my cattle prod and run the mother fuckers out. Now they're staying in the fucking stairways and I can't get to them. Run them the fuck out and this month's rent is paid."

"Consider it done," I told him.

Rodney wheeled himself to a board on a wall that had around fifty keys hanging on hooks. He tossed me one. "Good to have you back," he told me. "The place ain't been the same without you."

"I wish I could say it was good to be back," I told Rodney.

He laughed. "Yeah, I heard that," he said.

CHAPTER 9

I went by and took a look at the old place before collecting my suitcases and Tom. Everything was the same. Even my office sign: John Dark Detective, Open Every Day, was still nailed to the outside of the door.

Maybe Rodney had been expecting me to come back. Well, you can take the boy out of the ghetto but you can't take the ghetto out of the boy. This boy can't seem to stay the fuck out of the ghetto.

Everything was dusty as hell. That was to be expected. I slapped the back of the couch and a cloud puffed up and circled around my head. Bits of dust particles stung my eyes.

The ice box was unplugged and completely bare except for an old bottle of Ancient Age Whiskey. I was glad the ice box was empty. Anything in there would have been growing for months.

I plugged in the fridge. The light came on. I unscrewed the lid to the bottle of Ancient Age and smelled the whiskey inside. It smelled terrible, just the way it's supposed to.

The bedroom was the same. The same blankets and sheets were thrown over the bed. I'd dust them out later, if ever.

The bathroom was the same. No one had left me a gift in the toilet. I didn't need to take a crap so I left.

As I was closing the door to the apartment behind me I took a good look at my new/old home. Everything inside was old and tattered. Even the old Philco black and white TV I'd had before was there.

Home Sweet Home.

Fuck it! It'll do.

*   *   *

On the way down to the Porsche to get Tom and my bags I woke up the two drunks and told them they were going to have to leave.

They stared at me with red rimmed bleary eyes. One of them was a tall skinny white guy with stringy greasy black hair. The other was a fat Mexican guy.

The white guy yelled, "Fuck you!"

I stepped over them and said, "I'm moving my stuff in. When I get back, be gone or I'm going to throw your asses down these stairs."

They were on the second floor landing. There were enough stairs between the second and first floor to make the trip unpleasant.

Out on the street I had to run off two teenagers who were trying to stick a coat hanger through the window to pop the door lock. I knew I'd have to park this car somewhere else otherwise this shit was going to happen every day.

It's sure great to be back home.

Tom was half asleep in his carrier. He looked like he'd decided to just make the best of his imprisonment. I grabbed the two suitcases from the trunk and grabbed Tom's cat carrier and headed back up the steps.

The two drunks were still on the second floor landing waiting for me. I told them to get the fuck out of my way and that as soon as I dropped this shit off I was coming back to beat the hell out of them.

The Mexican laughed and showed rows of black and brown teeth. The white guy lifted his leg and ripped out a long loud wet sounding fart.

"That's what I think of you telling us to mother-fucking leave," He slurred at me.

Tom was wide awake now. He clawed at the wire mesh door to his carrier and hissed like a pissed off cobra.

"What the fuck you gonna do," the white guy laughed at me, "Sick your pussy on us?"

I looked at Tom through the door to his carrier and he was staring at the white guy with fury in his eyes. What the fuck, I thought. You know the neighborhood. Besides, I just wanted to see what the hell would happen.

Setting the suitcases and the cat carrier down at the same time I flipped the door open to Tom's carrier.

Moving faster than I thought anything could move, Tom screeched and yowled and tore out of the carrier, climbed the white guy's legs, and was on his chest tearing at his face in less than three seconds.

The drunk screamed and stumbled backward falling on the stairs and bashed the back of his skull a good one.

Tom jumped off when the drunk went down and stood at the man's feet with his back hair standing up making a loud rrrrrllll sound that made the hairs on the back of my neck stand up.

The drunk had two matching deep scratches on both cheeks that were already starting to drip blood down his face.

"I'm sorry, goddamn it! Call that little mother-fucker off," the white guy said, backing away from Tom, hugging the railing.

"We're fucking gone," the Mexican said and both of them went around us and down the stairs.

As soon as they were out of sight, I sat down on the stairs. Tom came and sat beside me and stared in my eyes the same way he'd done back in Sherry's apartment.

"You're full of all kinds of surprises ain't you," I told him.

He went mrooow.

I picked up the suitcases and told him, "Let's go home dude. You've earned yourself some tuna tonight."

That seemed to please him.

CHAPTER 10

I dropped the suitcases inside the door to my apartment and Tom followed me inside. He immediately headed for the window.

His litter box was still in its place beneath the window. He jumped in, made a few circles, scratched at the litter and started squeezing off a big fat tomcat turd.

He knew he was home.

I opened the window over his box and looked down. Winos were sprawled around lying in the alley passing a bottle around. I thought about yelling down that they better find another spot for their siestas. This is where I dump Tom's litter box when it gets full. Then I thought, to hell with it. They'll find out the hard way that I'm back.

After scratching Tom on the head while he was still taking a dump, I left the window open and headed back downstairs. I wasn't worried about leaving the window open for Tom to come and go as he pleased.

He was the kind of cat that went wherever the hell he wanted to. He always came back because he wanted to, not because he was caged up. As far as worrying about burglars, the way this building was built only a cat or Spiderman could get in my window.

My cat could come and go as he wanted.

Spiderman wasn't tough enough to come to East St. Louis. So I didn't worry about him.

* * *

On the street beside my Porsche a fight was about to break out.

Johnny Davis was facing off with two young idiots who were getting ready to put a brick through my window.

Just as I came out the door the bigger guy yelled at Johnny, "This ain't yo' mother-fucking car! Whatever we want to take, we gonna mother-fucking take!"

"You ain't taking shit boy!" Johnny yelled back.

"Hey boy!" I shouted. "That is my fucking car. You back the fuck off or I will fuck you up."

"Fuck you!" He yelled back.

I was pissed off and wanted to kill something. After this week, I was long overdue. Out of habit I reached for my gun.

Shit!

I didn't even have a goddamned holster on, much less a gun. I'd been without wearing it for so long I didn't even have the habit anymore.

"Are you looking for one of these?" Johnny asked and pulled a snub-nosed .38 out from under his coat and handed it to me. "When I heard what happened, I figured you'd need a gun and I knew you'd need me."

The snub-nose felt good in my hand, heavy, just like the chunk of killing steel that it was.

Johnny pulled out a gleaming chrome plated .45 and held it down at his side. We looked at the two guys who had been giving Johnny trouble, but they were already trotting across the street to get the hell away from us.

The sight of the two guns, in the hands of two men mean enough to use them, changed these boys' minds about being bad asses.

I looked at the gun in my hand and then at Johnny. "Thanks bro," I told him. "You were right on time."

"I always am," he said, "And I ought to kick your fucking ass for not calling me. We're friends' goddamn it and don't you ever forget that."

I felt all choked up inside but in East St. Louis only the bitches cry. Instead I said, "We got some son-of-a-bitches to kill. I just don't know who yet."

"That's the way I like hearing you talk," Johnny said. "Let's go find out who needs to die."

We both climbed into the Porsche and drove away.

CHAPTER 11

The first order of business was switching out the Porsche with my old Olds Delta 88. Where I was living now I'd have to be guarding the Porsche twenty four hours a day or that car would go to pieces in no time.

We drove over the McKinley Bridge and headed to the parking lot behind Patty's Kitten House to do the switch.

On the way Johnny asked, "So what have you done so far? If I know you, you ain't just been sitting around beating your meat."

I told him about the way Sherry looked when I identified her body, and checking out the sight where she was found, and questioning the guys at the liquor store and the porno shop.

"My next plan," I said to Johnny, "Is to look up the people I used to do business with. I figure this has got to be someone with a grudge against me that took it out on Sherry."

We had just arrived at the gate to the parking lot at Patty's Kitten House and Johnny stopped me before I got out of the Porsche to open the padlock and swing open the gate.

"You're dead wrong Bro." He told me.

"Come again?"

"I doubt this had shit to do with you," Johnny said. "One thing I've known about you for years is that you carry a big load of guilt on your head all the time. You tend to think anything bad happens in this world, it had to be your fault somehow. You're too close to Sherry to be objective. Now I liked Sherry but I can still think about this from the outside. The people you did your dealings with, they'd kill you for a buck and a half. But torture? That wouldn't make any sense from those kinds of dudes.

Sherry was a beautiful woman and she wasn't raped. Whoever killed her was trying to get some information."

I thought about that for a moment then said, "You're probably right."

"Ain't no probably to it," Johnny said. "I know I'm right and so do you."

*   *   *

We had to jump start my ancient Olds Delta 88 and when it finally kicked over the tailpipe belched out a cloud of smoke. The entire time I was attaching the jumper cables to the cars and juicing up the battery, my mind was working on what Johnny had said.

When we got in the Olds and left the parking lot of Patty's Kitten House behind, I drove us back to my apartment. We had a box of financial records and a few old personal contacts to check out.

*   *   *

In the apartment, the first place Johnny went to was to my refrigerator. He looked at it being empty, except for the bottle of Ancient Age whiskey, and said, "I can see you're all set up for some nutritious meals."

"I got everything in there I need," I told Johnny and it was right then that my stomach made a rumbling noise. It was getting to be two in the afternoon and those two breakfast burritos from McDonalds were a distant memory.

"Why don't you run out and get us some food?" I said to Johnny. "We'll be able to check this stuff out while we're eating something."

"I ain't your mother fucking gopher," Johnny said.

"Look, I buy, you fly."

"All right, I'm in the mood for some White Castle Burgers. Those sound good to you?"

"Yeah, I always like those," I told Johnny. "But I thought they gave you the runs."

"They do, but I've been kind of stopped up lately. Feels like I'm carrying a ten pound bag of cement around with me. Those babies ought to loosen everything up."

He got up and I gave him some money.

"And pick me up a few cans of tuna, too," I told him.

At the mention of the word tuna Tom came striding across the floor to us.

"Damn, he even knows what the word means," Johnny said.

Tom gave Johnny a look that said, "Who you think is fucking stupid?"

I told Johnny about Tom running off the drunks.

"Shit, you a mean little mother fucker, ain't you," Johnny told Tom and kneeled down and scratched the top of his head.

Tom purred.

He was making out good today.

CHAPTER 12

Johnny went for the White Castles and I grabbed the box of financial records to go through.

Most of what was in the box was the usual stuff, receipts for power bills, light bulbs, liquor, advertising, things like that. I glanced through it. Then I got the ledger from Sherry's check book and started matching that to the receipts.

I'm not sure why I was doing this. It really just seemed to be something to do. Sherry kept her bills paid. I wasn't going to find out someone murdered her because a payment was overdue for her janitorial service.

Then I saw something that didn't make any sense. There was a payment written in and dated for the day that Sherry was murdered. The check was for twenty thousand dollars and it was made out to a William Po.

Twenty Thousand dollars?

That's a lot of money to be paying to anyone in one lump sum. If Sherry was buying something for that much I'd have to figure I'd have known something about it.

We were working at the same place and were living together too.

Right then Johnny arrived with a dozen White Castle Burgers.

I showed him the entry for the twenty thousand dollars.

"Yeah, I'd have to figure that's unusual." He said.

We broke open the burgers and attacked them, and went backwards through Sherry's bank records. My stomach was knotting up and it wasn't the White Castles that were causing it.

Six months earlier to the day another check for twenty thousand dollars was in the ledger for William Po. There was another one six months before that to the same person. That was as far back as that check book reached.

"We may have hit this on the head first try," I told Johnny.

"Yeah," he answered. "This does not look right."

We kept eating and kept looking. What we looked for next in the box was the cancelled checks to William Po.

I wasn't feeling very hungry by then and ate automatically shoving the little burgers in my mouth and chewing them up like a grinding machine.

Sherry kept everything in good order. It wasn't a problem at all finding two cancelled checks to William Po. All of Sherry's cancelled checks were in chronological order. We just went backward.

They were exactly where they were supposed to be inside a rubber banded stack.

Stamped across the front of the check was Bank of Tehan Setar.

"You ever heard of that bank?" I asked Johnny.

"Shit, I don't think so," he answered, "And it don't sound like no bank around here."

While Johnny crammed more White Castle burgers into his mouth, I got Sherry's cell phone from my jacket pocket and called Joe Briggs at the Police Department. I knew Joe was only a local cop with local connections but, what the hell, maybe he could get hold of someone who would know who this William Po is.

After the phone rang five times it went to his answering machine. I left the message, "Joe, this is Dark. Going through Sherry's records we came across the name of a William Po who we think is based in a place named Tehan Setar. Sherry was paying this guy some large sums of money. We don't know what it means yet. If you can find out anything about this guy let me know. I'll be at," I left Sherry's cell phone number on his machine.

I hung up.

*   *   *

At the second National bank where Sherry had her account I asked to see one of their account specialists. Johnny and me was shown to a large desk off to the side of the lobby and told someone would be with us in a few minutes.

We waited, listening to generic elevator music that would work really great as a sleep aid. The guy who showed up to help us was a young dude in his early twenties.

We shook hands and he asked us, "How may I help you gentlemen?"

I showed him one of the checks made out to William Po. "I need to know the address of where this payment went to," I told the clerk.

"And you are?" He asked.

"I'm John Dark," I answered.

"Uh…No," he said. "What I meant was who are you in relation to Miss Sherry St. Claire?"

"She's my woman," I answered.

"So you are married," he said.

"No, but we soon will be," I told him.

"Well," the young guy said. "I can tell you more than likely William Po is from Tehan Setar but that's all I can tell you."

"Look, I need to know where this money went to," I told the young guy, who was sitting there with the self-satisfied smirk on his face of someone who knows you need something, and he has the power to stop you from getting it. "I think this William Po cheated Sherry out of this money and I aim to get it back for her."

The smile never left the clerk's face. "Then Miss St. Claire will have to come in herself. We do not give out confidential information. If you were married, possibly, but just a boyfriend, I don't think so."

It was that "just a boyfriend," that got to me. That and the shit eating grin on his face.

I stood up and leaned over the desk toward Mr. Account Specialist. "What if I slapped you so fucking hard you shit down both legs?"

He leaned back in his chair.

I went on.

"Then I'd squeeze your balls till your eyes bulge out. Think you could give me that goddamned information then?"

He rolled his office chair back from the desk.

Johnny told me, "Woe boy, slow down! We ain't gonna get shit this way." He grabbed my arms and pulled me backward.

"Leave now," the young guy said, "Or I'll call security."

"Fuck you," I told him and Johnny pulled me toward the door.

When we were outside Johnny told me, "That sure as shit went real smooth didn't it."

"Well, fuck him. He's an idiot," I said.

"Yeah, maybe he is," Johnny told me, "But I'm doing most of the talking from now on. Man, you can't fucking control yourself."

CHAPTER 13

We headed to Johnny's Bar and Grill. I needed a quiet place to make a phone call from.

Johnny closed up for the day when Rodney called him and let him know I'd be living at my old place again. Johnny unlocked the door to his place and we went inside. His grandmother Jeanette was waiting for us at a candle lit table.

She stood when I walked up to her and gave me a big bear hug. "I am so sorry to hear about what happened to Sherry," Jeanette told me and her Cajun accented voice broke on the words. "I really liked that girl. She only did good for the people who knew her."

I started getting choked up too and hugged Jeanette back, but I couldn't allow myself to let go and let the pain take hold of me. I'd be no good at getting done what I had to get done if I allowed that to happen.

I pushed Jeanette away and took a step back. My voice was harsher than I wanted it to be. "Why don't you break out that fucking crystal ball Jeanette?" I told her. "I need to know who tortured my woman to death. They need to pay!"

Jeanette looked deeply into my eyes. She reached out a hand to touch my cheek. I turned away.

"I only wish I could," she said. "What I can touch is the spirit and supernatural realms. What happened to Sherry had nothing to do with any of that. She was touched by the evil that ordinary men create. Of that evil, I know no more than you do."

"That's fucking great," I told her.

"She's just being truthful," Johnny told me.

"Yeah," I said. "But right now the truth ain't doing shit."

*   *   *

I got Sherry's cell phone from my jacket pocket and dialed Nash Graham, the head of the DEA in the Midwestern United States. Graham was the kind of guy who had contacts in practically everything. I'd done some jobs for him that were not even close to being legal, so I figured I'd make use of his information network for a change.

Where it was a question as to whether or not Joe Briggs could get any information on William Po, the only way Nash Graham would come up dry was if William Po didn't exist.

On the second ring a secretary answered.

"I need to speak to Nash Graham," I told her.

"And what is your business with Mr. Graham?" She asked.

"Just tell him John Dark called and to call me back immediately at," I reeled off Sherry's cell number.

"I need to know your business please," the secretary asked again.

I spoke slowly. "Tell him John Dark called." I hung up.

Thirty seconds later the phone rang.

I flipped the phone open.

"What do you need, John?" Graham said without even saying who he was.

I told him about what happened to Sherry.

"I'm real sorry to hear that," Graham told me, but the tone of voice he used let me know that I might as well have told him that my favorite football team just lost. Basically, he didn't know Sherry so he didn't give a shit.

"I need to have you check out a name and let me know whatever you find out about it. The name is William Po. I think he's from a place named Tehan Setar."

Graham cut me off with, "I can't use company resources for personal matters. I'm sorry but…"

I cut him off, "Remember a little while back when you hired me to eliminate a certain cross dresser who black mailed your son into suicide? I think I'd call that a personal matter and I know you didn't pay me out of your own pocket."

"Look John, I can't," Graham said.

"Look Graham," I told him. "You either come up with something about this guy or these news reporters who want to talk to me are going to get a long story about DEA chiefs who cover their own asses by hiring people like me to kill for them."

"Are you threatening me? Because if you are I'll send some boys after you to…"

I cut him off again, "I don't give a fuck about you," I told Graham. "Make some phone calls. Use your contacts and just let me know who this guy is. You do this for me and I'll do the next job you want for free."

"You're damn right you will," Graham said. "Besides, I thought you were retired."

"Not anymore," I told him. "The reason I retired is dead."

There was silence on the line between us for ten long seconds then Graham said, "OK. I'll find out whatever I can on William Po from Tehan Setar. You owe me one."

"I always pay my debts," I told him.

"You'll pay me," he said and hung up.

CHAPTER 14

As soon as the phone disconnected the silence in Johnny's Bar and Grill fell over us like a heavy blanket. Johnny had locked the front door behind us so no customers could come in. Jeanette went upstairs to the apartment she was sharing with Johnny to do whatever the hell it is that grandmothers do.

I looked at Johnny.

He looked at me.

"Well, what the fuck do we do now?" I asked.

"Not much I figure we can do right now," Johnny answered. "We gotta wait for Graham or Joe to call us back with some info."

"I can't just wait," I told him. "I'll go insane after about five minutes if I just sit around."

"Let's go out then," Johnny said. "A couple beers will do us some good."

"I don't drink," I told Johnny.

"Why the fuck not?" Johnny asked. "You got someone waiting up for you?"

I gave Johnny a FUCK YOU! look.

"I'm sorry, bro," Johnny said. "My mouth over-ran my ass. I shouldn't have said that."

"No, you shouldn't have," I told him. "Problem is you're right."

We headed toward the door. Just as Johnny grabbed hold of the knob I said, "Wait a second. I need to make another call."

While Johnny waited I called Paul Harris. He answered on the second ring.

"John Dark here," I told him. "How are the arrangements for Sherry's funeral going?"

"Everything is set," he answered. "Day after tomorrow, eleven in the morning at St. Luke's on Sullivan Avenue. They want you there about ten to make sure all the arrangements are the way you want them."

"Everything will be ok," I told Paul. "I can't tell you how much I appreciate you doing this."

Paul said, "You don't have to. This is not an easy time for you. I also found notes that you had Kira Brooks and Lisa Rios buried at Pine Bluff Cemetery and took the liberty of buying a plot over there for Sherry."

Two women who had been in my life were in the ground in Pine Bluff. Soon another would be. If things kept going like this the women in John Dark's life would have their own section in that graveyard.

I must have been silent for too long because Paul said, "If you want to I can change that. Any of these arrangements can be changed."

"No, that's fine," I told him.

We said our good-byes and hung up.

I looked at Johnny.

"Let's go get a buzz," he said. "We both need it."

I couldn't have agreed more.

*   *   *

A light dusting of snow was starting to fall as we climbed into my old Olds Delta 88. The wind was raw and the temperature was dropping. The entire St. Louis metropolitan area was getting set to be put into the deep freeze. The weather fit me like a glove. With what had happened to Sherry my world would never be a warm place again.

It took a few minutes for the car to warm up. Sitting unused for the better part of a year hadn't done this old motor any good. After wheezing and coughing for about ten minutes I was finally able to make the car roll away from the curb.

We breathed heavy grey clouds inside the car that fogged the windshield up. The defroster wasn't for shit and neither was the heater. As the car coughed on down the road I just kept wiping the windshield with my hand and kept on driving.

Johnny didn't even ask me where I was driving to. We both pretty much like the same kind of things, and since we weren't choir boys it was a sure bet I wasn't taking us to a Baptist Revival Meeting.

The roads were not slick…yet. The snow was drifting down like the ash from a heaven burned away. Last week I was living in heaven and didn't even know it. This week everything inside me was burned away.

Johnny wasn't surprised when I traced the roads to the outskirts of East St. Louis and pulled into the parking lot of a little strip club named Roxie's.

Alcohol and loose women and sex without meaning, make that life without meaning, that's all that is left for me now.

That, and revenge.

They say revenge is sweet. I don't even give a fuck about that. I just want the bastards who hurt Sherry to feel as much pain as I have. Then I want them to feel nothing at all forever. Just like me.

The only difference between them and me is that I'll still be breathing.

CHAPTER 15

The flickering neon signs outside Roxie's gave the place a carnival atmosphere. I didn't feel like celebrating but we went in anyway. At the door the bouncer recognized me and told me how sorry he was about Sherry's death, then waved us past without charging us the cover of five dollars each.

Inside lights were blinking, music was pounding and women were gyrating like snakes on speed on the stages. I looked around the room and saw a lot of familiar faces from some of the regulars at Patty's Kitten House.

The majority of the men here were lonely guys who worked hard all week long just to go home to an empty house. Most of them didn't have a chance in hell of ever scoring with the women they were staring at. They'd go home later and think about these women and beat their meat. I guess whatever gets you through the night is what you've got to do.

We went and sat at a table and I realized that I didn't want to be at Roxie's. My woman's body was being prepared to be put in the ground in a day and a half. When I looked at the women on the stages bending over in front of guys, spreading their legs, giving them a peek, it all seemed so unimportant, so trivial. None of this meant anything.

Johnny waved at a waitress who let him know that she'd be over pretty soon. He saw the look on my face.

"We need to get you something to drink," he said.

"I shouldn't be here," I told him. "This ain't working for me."

"Maybe not," Johnny answered. "But what the fuck else you gonna do?"

The waitress came over and told me how sorry she was about Sherry and took our order. I was certain I was going to be hearing a lot of sorry's tonight.

When we went to pay for the drinks the waitress waved at the bartender who waved back.

"For you guys, it's on the house tonight," she said.

"Thanks," I told her.

We changed our order and I had her bring me four shots of Jack Daniels and a Budweiser. Johnny had four shots and a Jack and Coke.

The drinks came.

The waitress gave me a hug.

I picked up a shot.

Johnny picked up a shot. We clinked glasses and knocked it back.

It tasted like molten lava going down my throat. Just the way I wanted it to.

Music played.

Dancers danced.

People wandered by our table one by one and paid their respects each one telling me how much they liked Sherry and would miss her. I didn't know how much more of that I could take. It was like having a knife shoved in and twisted.

I downed two more shots. Johnny matched me. He probably wouldn't have any problem keeping up with me tonight. Johnny was in practice and I wasn't.

Drinking hard liquor is like any other sport. If you don't train for it, you don't do it too well.

The music changed to some kind of Congo sounding shit and the D.J. barked out over the PA system, "Gentlemen, start your engines, and if you can't get 'em started, here's the Amazon Queen. She's here to get you all revved up and ready to roar just like the king of the jungle. From deepest darkest Africa, put your hands together for Candi Divine!"

The D.J. was playing up that African angle real good. A little fantasy never hurt a sales pitch one bit. Candi was from Chicago, but nobody wanted to hear that.

The guys in the place gave Candi a decent round of applause.

Johnny turned to me and said, "Shit! I've seen this show one time too many."

Candi Divine was tall, long legged, had deep coffee brown skin and large breasts. Candi had muscles on top of muscles. Shit, that girl had been working out. She was strong! Candi was scary as a mother-fucker, too, because she had a man's package between her legs.

The guys around this place must have gotten used to Candi because the last time I'd been here most of them were even afraid to look in her direction. Now she actually got a few of them to wander up and stick bills in her G-string. She'd pat them on the head and mouth, "Thank-you," back at them.

She was doing body building poses and slow motion martial arts strikes to the beat of the music. Candi wasn't my type of woman but she was impressive as hell.

When Candi was dancing to the last song in her set a guy walked in. He waved at us, and strode directly to the stage where Candi was doing her thing.

It was that big corn-fed, blond-haired, country boy, ex-pro football player that worked at Patty's Kitten House, Ron Martin.

Ron pulled a bill from his pocket and folded it lengthwise a few times until it looked like a long green cigarette. Then he stuck it in his mouth. He leaned his face forward and Candi squatted down and pressed her breasts to both sides of Ron's face.

"Shit," Johnny said. "Does he know what the fuck he's getting into?"

"I really don't know," I answered him, "And I don't give a fuck either."

Ron looked like he was having a real good time. When Candi pulled back a little bit to take the bill from between his teeth he let the bill go then grabbed Candi by both tits (one in each hand) and kissed the nipples on both of them.

Candi stood up with an expression of open-mouthed surprise on her face. Then she smiled a big smile, squatted down in front of Ron again, wrapped her arms around his head, and gave him a big tongue dancing, open mouthed kiss.

"Shit," Johnny said. "That's fucking disgusting,"

"He doesn't seem to mind," I said, and Ron did seem to be having fun.

After they broke off the embrace and Candi continued dancing while fanning herself to cool down, Ron Martin left the stage area and came over and pulled up a chair at our table.

"How are you holding up John?" He asked me and we shook hands.

"I'll never be the same," I told him. "But I'll survive."

"Yeah," he said. "I can't believe anybody would do that to Sherry."

Johnny said to Ron, "Man, I got to ask you, you do know that Candi has got balls right?"

Ron laughed. "Candi impressed me right off the bat as being a woman that's got a whole lot of spunk."

"You could say that," Johnny told him. "What I'm trying to tell you is that that woman ain't no woman. You go hunting for beaver with her, you gonna feel nuts."

Ron was smiling but he sounded serious to me when he said, "Don't be talking about my girlfriend. I know everything there is to know about her."

"Evidently not enough," Johnny started.

Ron stopped him from talking by asking, "You ever seen Spartacus?"

"Shit, we met that mother-fucker," Johnny said.

"No," Ron said. "I'm talking about the movie. There's a scene where this Roman General comes on to a slave played by Tony Curtis. He asks him, 'Do you like oysters or clams?' Well, I like them both."

"Yeah, I remember that," Johnny said. "So what the fuck does sea food got to do with this?"

"Let me put it like this," Ron Martin said, "so someone even as thick as you can get it. I'd have fucked them both."

Johnny gave Ron a strange look. "You ain't saying…" He couldn't finish the statement.

Ron laughed. "Candi's got exactly what I need." He said. "With her, I get the bonus plan."

"Shit," Johnny said. "And a big strapping white boy like you, too. Ain't that a bitch."

Ron laughed.

Fur Elise began playing in my jacket pocket. The cell phone was ringing. I pulled it out and flipped it open.

"Saved by the bell," I told Ron and Johnny.

CHAPTER 16

It was Joe Briggs on the telephone. "Something's come up," Joe told me. "I need you to meet me somewhere right now."

"Is this about William Po?" I asked. "Did you find out anything?"

"Nothing to do with Po," Briggs answered. "Come out to where Bunkum Road intersects Highway 157. I'll be waiting for you."

"What'd you find out?" I asked again.

"Can't say over the phone," Joe answered. "Just get out here."

He hung up.

I stood up and told Johnny, "Time to go."

"Good," Johnny said. "This shit was getting boring anyway."

Candi had finished her set and came over, draped her arms around Ron's shoulders, and kissed him on the neck.

They made a cute couple: the all American Football Hero and the Jet Black African Amazon Queen with color coordinated dicks and balls. Hey, whatever works for them is all right. The way my relationships go I'll probably never want to care about anyone ever again.

Ron stood up and we shook hands one more time. "If you need anything," he said. "Especially taking care of whoever hurt Sherry, you let me know. I want a piece of that meat too."

"I'll remember that," I told him and me and Johnny left.

*   *   *

On the way over to where 157 crosses Bunkum Road, which is just outside of Washington Park and Caseyville, I filled Johnny in on what I knew, which was that I didn't know anything.

Joe wouldn't say anything over the phone so we'd have to wait until we got there to find out anything at all.

It was dark outside and the snow was coming down heavier than when we'd entered Roxie's. It wasn't anywhere close to a blizzard yet, but with as cold as it was, all the snow that was falling would stick to the ground and make everything slick.

My Olds Delta 88 started up quicker than it had earlier in the day and the motor warmed up faster. Maybe it was loosening up a bit after sitting for so long. As we turned onto Bunkum Road the defroster got warm enough to actually do a little bit of good.

The heater still wouldn't do shit but blow out cold air. I left it off and cruised through the falling snow.

The white flakes drifting down from the black sky made it seem peaceful and quiet out in the world. Too bad that's not the way it really was.

We cruised over the frozen road mostly in silence. I got to admit I wasn't much for conversation lately. Life was weighing me down. It wasn't easy to make light chit chat when you feel like you're swimming in the ice cold muddy Mississippi wearing a lead overcoat.

Where 157 crossed Bunkum Road was a fenced in Park-N-Ride lit by yellow fluorescent lights. It was the only thing out here. That's where I pulled into.

The yellow lights made the falling snow look like tiny flames falling down from heaven. Too bad it didn't make the place any warmer.

Joe Briggs recognized my car when I pulled into the lot. He got out and waved me over. The Park-N-Ride was pretty much deserted, only a few empty cars in spots waiting for their owners to drive them home after work.

I pulled into the parking spot beside Joe Briggs car and got out. Johnny got out.

Before I even got to Joe's open window he said to the two of us, "Follow me."

"What's this about?" I asked him again.

"You'll find out when we get there."

We got back in the car.

Joe slowly rolled on ahead of us crunching the snow beneath his tires. He left the Park-N-Ride and went East on Bunkum Road. I followed the red dots of his tail lights.

*   *   *

After about ten miles on Bunkum Road, Joe turned off onto another smaller road that was dark and lined on both sides by trees. After a mile on that one he turned off again onto a gravel road.

I don't remember the names of those last two roads and even if I did I wouldn't name them here. There are some places that have to always remain a secret.

The red tail lights on Joe's car bounced ahead of us for about a mile more, then he pulled onto a driveway and after fifty yards he pulled up to an old looking small cinderblock house.

We pulled up beside his car and got out. Another car, a late model sedan was already parked out front.

A few lights were shining out through windows with drawn curtains.

Joe Briggs got out of his car and came to the front of it, and with snow swirling around his head he sat down on the hood.

"All right man," I said to Joe. "It's time you told us what the hell's going on here."

Joe looked at Johnny, "Are you ready to be involved in some ugly shit?" he asked. "What I got here isn't going to be pretty."

Johnny answered. "Sherry was my friend. I'll do whatever I have to do to make the people who killed her pay."

"Just wanted to get that clear," Joe said. He looked from Johnny to me. "The man we got inside, we've been following for a long time. He runs video tapes of kiddy porn between East St. Louis and Kansas City. We got his name from a pedophile in exchange for a lighter sentence. We don't know who he makes his pickups from or who he delivers to. On a routine traffic stop tonight, the officer inside this house searched his car without reading this piece of shit his rights. So he'll walk if he makes it to court."

"What's this got to do with us?" I asked Joe.

Joe looked hard into my eyes. He said, "While we were holding him we went through the tapes he has, one of them is a tape of Sherry's murder."

CHAPTER 17

I went through the front door of the small cinder block house with my head buzzing. The cold and snow seemed to be on another plane of existence from the rest of my body. I didn't feel anything. I was like a machine, a machine of destruction.

The inside of the house had blank white walls and uncovered cement floors. There was only one large central room to the place. A young cop sat on a folding chair in front of a small table that had a TV/VCR combo set up on it. He was watching *Wheel of Fortune*.

I wasn't here for any games.

Across the room was a large cage. It was a portable cell. I knew what this place was. This was a secluded location where the cops brought criminals to beat information out of them.

Inside the cage was a stocky middle aged white man in a business suit. He reminded me of Donald Trump only not quite as self-confident. He was looking very nervous. He had every right to be.

Against the large white wall were two large card board boxes. The tops of the boxes were open. The boxes were filled with video tapes.

Joe Briggs told the young cop to go home and to never tell anyone about where he had been tonight.

"You don't have to worry about that," the young cop said. "Whatever this asshole gets, he deserves."

The young cop left.

The guy inside the cage was sitting on the floor leaning his back against the bars.

Joe Briggs walked directly to him. He said through the bars, "Are you ready to talk yet? If not, I got someone I'm going to introduce you to."

"Anything I've got to say, I'll say to my lawyer," the guy answered him.

"Let me see the video tape," I said to Joe.

He walked over to the boxes of tapes and took one sitting on top. On the white label was written "S. St. Claire".

Johnny walked up to the bars of the cage and took one in each hand. "You are in a world of hurt," he told the guy inside. "I advise you to tell us everything we want to know."

"Speak to my lawyer," the man said.

"Shit," Johnny told the man. "Ain't no lawyer on Earth gonna help you tonight."

I popped the tape in the TV/VCR combo. It instantly went to play.

Johnny spoke again. "You were carrying a snuff film. That man over there," Johnny pointed at me, "Is the meanest son-of-a-bitch I've ever met. He was going to marry the woman in that movie."

I heard the man suck in his breath. He was scared. Good! I wanted him to be frightened.

Why is it that a man feels the need to experience pain? I knew what was on that tape was going to tear the guts out of me, but I had to see it anyway. Maybe, that's exactly why I had to see it.

Sherry was carried in naked and unconscious over the shoulder of a guy in a black rubber mask and rain coat. She was sat down onto a wooden chair and her arms were bound behind her back.

There was a table beside the chair with all kinds of shop tools. These tools were never designed to be used on living flesh.

The guy in the rubber mask picked up something small off the table and appeared to snap it in half under Sherry's nose. It must have been smelling salts.

Sherry coughed and wheezed and her eyes flew open. The man in the mask leaned over and looked in Sherry's face. "You are a beautiful woman," he said. "I will not destroy your beauty." His voice was low and raspy. It sounded like it came from the lower pits of hell.

"Where is William Po?" the man asked.

"I do not know a William Po," Sherry answered. "Is this someone I should know?"

The man picked up a ball peen hammer from the table and slammed it down upon Sherry's unprotected thigh.

Sherry screamed and it tore through my brain. My stomach tightened and the coppery taste of blood came into my mouth.

When the sound of pain stopped echoing from the speakers the man spoke again. "Where is William Po?"

"I don't know!" Sherry screamed back at him.

He picked up a pair of pliers and with them grasped a piece of skin on Sherry's side and twisted.

The shriek that Sherry let out was blood curdling.

"No one will hear you," the man told her. "Tell us and we'll let you go. You don't know who we are. But I can keep doing this for hours." To demonstrate he grabbed one of her nipples with the pliers and twisted it savagely ripping the skin.

This was the same nipple that I had taken in my mouth more times than I could count. I felt sick to my stomach but couldn't stop watching.

Sherry screamed and passed out.

The man crushed another tablet of smelling salts under her nose and began again.

The same question was asked over and over and it always got the same answer. Sherry kept saying that she didn't know who they were talking about.

After about an hour another man entered the room.

This man was small and Asian. He was dressed in a Hawaiian style shirt and white slacks.

He went to Sherry and leaned over in front of her and looked into her pained eyes. She was barely conscious. Sherry had passed out from the pain five times. She now had all the wounds that I had seen on her at the morgue, except for one.

"You are a brave woman," the man told her, "But your suffering is for nothing. You, more than most people, should know that we cannot be fought. We are only businessmen who supply a product. Right or wrong does not exist, only profit. We will show this," he pointed directly at the camera, "As an example of those who work against us. We will find William Po and destroy him."

Sherry lifted her head and spit in the man's face.

He snatched a knife up from the table and cut Sherry's throat.

CHAPTER 18

As the blood cascaded down Sherry's naked breasts I hit the stop button on the VCR. The screen went blank. I ejected the tape and slid it into an inside jacket pocket.

I stood up from the chair. A strange dizziness came over me. It was almost like I couldn't feel the floor beneath my feet.

I picked up the chair and slid it over in front of where the bars were. The room was lit by two sets of harsh neon lights.

I turned to Joe. "Why were you keeping tabs on this piece of shit?" I asked.

"We keep track of everybody who's been accused of a sex crime. Mr. Arnold Jenkins here tried to molest a seven year old girl two years ago. Then his name turned up in a kiddy porn sting. Now, we got him with the goods."

"I want to call my lawyer right now," Arnold Jenkins said.

"Shut the fuck up!" I yelled at Jenkins.

To Joe I said, "I think it's time for you to leave. What's going to happen here will not be good for your police career."

Joe Briggs considered this for a moment and then he said, "I think you're right."

He clapped me on the back. "You boys can find your way out of here right?"

"Oh hell yeah," Johnny told him. "We're about to give this gentleman a guided tour of hell. We've been there already. So we know the way back."

When Joe reached the door Jenkins shouted at him, "I got the right to call my lawyer."

Joe looked over his shoulder and told him, "You just lost all your rights." Then to us, "Have fun. Someone will be by tomorrow to clean up the mess."

* * *

A peculiar calmness came over me. I sat down in the chair facing the bars.

Jenkins was standing up. He pointed at the TV/VCR combo. "I didn't have anything to do with that," he said.

"I didn't think you did," I told him.

"I…I just deliver this stuff and they pay me. That's all."

"I don't give a fuck," I told him. I pulled the snub nosed .38 out of my pocket.

"Hold on a second," Jenkins said. "You're just trying to scare me. Cops can't do this."

Johnny asked me, "Do we look like cops?"

"I'm beginning to think so," I answered.

I looked around the room for the key to the cage.

Jenkins said, "I'm not saying anything until my lawyer gets here."

The key was lying next to the TV/VCR combo. I picked it up.

"You just don't get it," I told Jenkins. "You're not getting out of this room alive."

I pointed my gun at him and Jenkins covered his face with his hands. I shot him in the right foot.

He shrieked falling to the floor. Thick crimson liquid pulsed between his fingers as he tried to hold together his ruined foot.

"Oh man," Johnny said, "That was fucked up! He sure ain't gonna be entering any tap dancing contests for a while."

I unlocked the cage door and stepped inside. "So, you like kids," I said to Jenkins.

Jenkins was sitting down hugging his foot as good as he could, "Oh god," he yelled. "Get me to a hospital!"

I kicked him where the blood was flowing. Red spurted into the air.

Jenkins screamed.

"Where'd you get the tapes?" I asked him.

"Get me to a hospital," Jenkins yelled again. A pool of blood was forming around him.

Johnny came to the bars. "Look man," Johnny said to Jenkins. "If you tell him what he wants to know, I think I can talk John into taking you to a doctor. If you don't, I ain't even gonna try."

I said to Jenkins, "Tell me this, you sack of shit, what the hell can you get out of fucking kids anyway? They're not even old enough to know what's happening to them."

Jenkins surprised the hell out of me by answering. He spoke as if he was proud of what he did. "It's doing something to them that they can't imagine is going to happen. The look in their eyes just before you stick it in is incredible. They can't believe it's going to happen."

I looked at Johnny.

He said, "This is a sick son-of-a-bitch we have here."

"This asshole has got to die," I said and took aim at Arnold Jenkins head.

He threw his hands up again kind of like he expected to catch the bullet being thrown at him. I shot the ring finger off of his left hand.

The scream he let out was deafening. I loved the sound of it.

When he had breath back in his lungs to speak, Jenkins asked, "Will you take me to a doctor if I tell you where I got the tapes from?"

"If you convince me what you say is true," I told him, "I'll let Johnny have a shot at talking me into it."

"All right, all right," Jenkins said. "Out on State Street and Fifth just outside East St. Louis is a porno shop. Ray's Triple X Gallery. I've been buying the tapes from him. He picks up kids off the streets and makes his own tapes in his basement. He's even let me in on making a few of them."

I knew the guy and I knew the place. I was already convinced.

Johnny asked him, "What's he do with the kids after he's done with them?"

"I don't know," Jenkins answered. "It's better in this kind of thing that you don't ask questions."

I stepped back from Jenkins.

"Let me out of here, OK. Get me to a doctor," he said.

I turned to Johnny.

"Well, John, can't you see what a wonderful guy we have here," Johnny said, "We really ought to help him out a bit, seeing how he is a pillar of the community and all. Hell, he's probably even a Boy Scout Master."

The thought of that turned my stomach.

"You tried, Johnny," I told him and stepped back outside the cage and locked the door. "But it just wasn't good enough."

Johnny said, "Shit dude, I tried. What can I say, John's a hard ass."

Jenkins yelled at us, "You can't leave me here like this. I'll bleed to death."

"That's the idea," I told him and shot him in the thigh.

We left to the sounds of his screams behind us. I considered going back and plugging a few more holes in Jenkins but that would make his end that much faster and I wanted him to die slow.

CHAPTER 19

My Olds Delta 88 chugged along the snow covered icy roads real nice. It's an old heavy steel boat of a car that has large tires that put a lot of rubber to the pavement. Now if I drive like an idiot I can definitely put this car in a ditch, but tonight I wasn't into driving crazy.

Tonight we were heading over to Ray's Triple X Gallery. I wanted us to get there in one piece.

We were on the outskirts of East St. Louis when Johnny told me, "You know I'm going to need to go in first."

"Why's that?"

"Well hell, he knows who you are," Johnny said. "After what you done to him he's probably keeping a gun under the counter, if he didn't have one before. You come waltzing in through his front door he'd blow your head off before you'd have a chance to scratch your balls."

"So, you got a plan?" I asked.

"Yeah," Johnny said. "Basically we wait until the last car leaves from in front of the place. I go in and check out the layout, find out if there's more than one guy in the store. At the same time you go around back and see if there's a back door and try it.

"If you can come in through the back that's great, if you can't, that's OK too because by then I'll have myself a spot where I can cover whoever is going to see you coming in through the front door.

"We get the drop on whoever's there whether there's one or two of them. We put the closed sign up and take them to a back room and make them tell us who made that tape with Sherry in it."

"What if they don't want to tell us?" I asked Johnny.

He laughed.

"Then," Johnny said, with a mean looking smile on his face, "The real horror show begins."

"That's exactly what I hoped you'd say," I told him.

*   *   *

We arrived at Ray's Triple X Gallery just after midnight. There were three cars parked in front, so we drove to the end of the block, past the only other open business, the liquor store, and parked back in the shadows.

About thirty yards away was the entrance to an alley that ran behind the buildings on this block, directly behind Ray's Triple X Gallery.

It was relatively quiet. Every now and then a car would pull up to the liquor store. Someone would go in then come back out a few minutes later with a package.

We sat far enough back in the shadows so that no one would notice the car idling as we waited.

After a while Johnny asked me, "What you gonna do when all this is over?"

"I don't know," I told him. "I'm not even thinking about that."

"Yeah, probably the best way to be," Johnny said. "Killing these guys ain't gonna bring Sherry back though."

"You don't think I know that?" I answered.

"I guess you do," he said. "So why are you doing this?"

"Cause there ain't a goddamned thing else I can do," I told Johnny.

"Guess not," he answered.

We sat and watched the snow come down out of the black sky.

Time passed.

The three cars stayed stationary in front of Ray's Triple X Gallery. The guys inside must have been taking turns blowing each other in the video booths. Nobody thumbs through magazines for hours on end.

Somewhere around two thirty the neon sign over the door to the liquor store flickered then went out. A small red neon sign, that we couldn't read, beside the door came on. A few seconds later the front door opened and the guy with stringy long brown hair that I'd talked to came out and locked up behind himself.

He walked to Ray's and went in through the front door.

A minute later two guys came out the front door and went to their cars.

I tapped Johnny on the shoulder. "Looks like it's almost show-time," I told him.

As the last word left my mouth another guy, a small guy, came out of the front door. He was helped along by a healthy shove from that tattooed headed idiot that I'd pulled over the counter and thrown to the floor.

The small guy stumbled and slid in the snow and almost went down.

He waved his arms and yelled something at Tattoo. From where we were we couldn't hear what he yelled.

Mr. Tattoo made a motion like he was going to go after the little guy and the little guy scurried to his car, got in, and reversed out of there.

As the disgruntled customer drove on down the road away from us, Mr. Tattoo went back inside his Triple X Gallery.

"Time to move," I told Johnny. "Give me five minutes then head on in."

"Sure thing," he answered.

I went out the car door and into the yawning mouth of the pitch black alley.

Stepping into that alley was like diving into a pool of oil. What light there was from the neon lights up front was completely cut off by the stone walls between them and where I was.

The darkness was complete. I couldn't even see my hand in front of my face and the ground seemed like it was miles away.

I pulled the snub nosed .38 and kept it down by my side. With my left hand I felt out in front of me like a blind man and moved forward into the dark.

The walls of the buildings on both sides were just vague dark shapes, only blackness against a slightly less pitch blackness behind them.

I moved forward down the alley feeling my way along with some kind of senses that I didn't even know I possessed, and was feeling pretty good about how well I was doing in the dark when I walked full into a big steel dumpster.

There was no way of knowing how far I had come or how close I was to the back of Ray's Triple X Gallery in the dark. It hit me at that moment that I had no idea which back door would be The Gallery's door. Hell, even if they

71

had marked the names of the businesses on the doors I didn't even have so much as a cigarette lighter to read what was wrote on them.

I was fucked!

Lights flashed on ahead momentarily blinding me.

I was glad as hell that I was behind the dumpster I'd banged into.

I crouched down and in a few seconds my eyes adjusted and I peeked around the side of the dumpster.

*   *   *

Johnny later told me what happened around front. This is what went down.

Getting out of the rider's side door onto the icy sidewalk, Johnny slipped and damn near busted his ass with the first step that he took.

He walked past the liquor store and saw that the small neon in the window was a closed sign.

He trudged on through the snow and got to Ray's Triple X Gallery just as the closed sign came on in the front window of that place.

Johnny tried the door anyway and it was locked. He banged on the door and yelled, "Hey! Your sign says open twenty four hours mother-fucker! Open the goddamned door!"

He kicked on the door and grabbed the iron mesh grill and shook it like a gorilla wanting out of his cage. Except, this gorilla wanted in.

Somebody yelled from inside, "We're closed. Get the fuck out of here before I come out there and kick your ass!"

Johnny yelled back, "Mother-fucker I need some K.Y. Jelly and I need it now! My old lady is ready to fuck but she's dry as the Sahara. Shit, I'll pay double price. I ain't gonna be humping no hole that feels like a goddamned cheese grater. If I don't get this K.Y. tonight, I swear I'll come back here tomorrow and I'll dry fuck you, you sorry ass bastard!"

Johnny was always real suave about getting his way.

CHAPTER 20

Around back I crouched low and peeked around the edge of the dumpster, seeing that a van had just pulled around the edge of the building and stopped with its lights on. I couldn't move anywhere because if I did, whoever was driving the van couldn't help but see me almost directly in front of where he was parked.

I stayed crouched down and waited.

A few seconds, which seemed like hours, the driver got out of the van and slammed the door behind him. Someone got out of the rider's side door too.

It was just my luck that they left the van idling with its lights pointing straight at where I was. In the glare of the headlights, trying to peek around the dumpster, I couldn't see shit except for the snowflakes falling between me and the van.

I heard someone open the rear doors of the van and shout, "Get your asses out here!"

I heard the sounds of shuffling and sniffling and a pitiful sound that was like the sound of frightened children sobbing.

A rusty door hinge creaked and I could hear muted shouting coming from inside.

"What the fuck is going on up there?" One of the guys who got out of the van yelled to whoever was inside as he came through the door.

A muted answer was shouted back from the inside, "Some fucking asshole wants to get in and won't go away."

I took a chance and stuck my head out far enough around the side of the dumpster to see around the van's headlights.

I couldn't see a whole hell of a lot because the light was still blinding me but I did see the outline of an open door and the vague outline of two men and three smaller shapes.

There was no way I could stay where I was and let that door close and lock behind them.

I charged the van running in a crouch and stopped just at the front of it, kneeling down between the two headlights.

* * *

Out front Johnny heard the guy inside yell, "I'm gonna give you to the count of five to get the fuck out of here or I'm coming out there to stomp you into the fucking pavement."

Johnny shouted back, "Five mother-fucker! Ten! Fifteen! Twenty! Get your monkey-ass out here! Talk shit to me. I will fuck you up, you son-of-a-bitch!"

* * *

Around back, Johnny was making so much noise that the two guys, who now I saw were leading three raggedy kids by a rope, just walked in through the door and left it wide open behind them.

I darted for it and caught the outside handle just before it swung shut on its own.

I swung the door open, stepped inside, and crouched low with my snub nose in my fist. At the far end of an aisle of video booths, the two guys were pushing the three kids in front of them.

The scent of stale cum was heavy in the air as was the grinding sounds of techno-rock screeched from speakers.

For whatever reason, I'll never know, when they reached the end of the hall and the first guy pulled back a curtain to enter the main part of the store, the guy behind glanced backward over his shoulder and saw me racing toward him.

He yelled, "What the fuck!" and dove into one of the video booths.

The other guy knocked the kids out of his way and dove to the side into the store.

I crouched and ducked into a video booth just as the first guy stuck his arm out and fired blindly into the hall.

*   *   *

Out front Johnny heard the shots and knew he had to get inside and fast. He jerked his chrome plated .45 out and, seeing the large painted over plate glass window, he blasted three shots into it and turned it into a pile of sharp, glittering, broken shards of glass.

He leaped through where the window had been, ready to shoot anything that moved. The window sill had only been knee high but it was high enough so that Johnny slid on the glass on the tile floor from the window and fell into a display of dildos and lubricants of all colors and flavors.

The display collapsed and Johnny fell right over the top of it.

His falling actually saved his life.

Ray, the tattooed headed wonder, had a sawed off shotgun in his hands and he fired a blast that went over Johnny's head as he was going down.

Johnny blindly fired two shots into the glass display case counter that Ray was behind and Ray went down.

*   *   *

The shots in the tight hallway made my ears ring, but I could hear well enough to know when the guy in that video booth stopped firing bullets and started clicking on empty chambers.

I jumped out of the booth I was in and sent two shots into the booth that I figured the guy shooting at me was in.

He screamed from inside his booth, "Oh god, I'm hit! It fucking hurts!"

The sound of his voice told me exactly where he was. I ran to the booth and just as I got there he yelled, "I fucking give up. Take me to jail."

"Too fucking late," I yelled back and pumped two shots through the clothe curtain into the booth.

He didn't make another sound.

*   *   *

In the front of the store Johnny scrambled around on the floor trying to find some cover behind a rack of triple X gay porno tapes.

"Who the fuck are these guys?" The other guy who'd come in from the van yelled.

"I don't fucking know," Ray yelled from behind the counter.

"Police!" Johnny yelled back. "You are all under arrest. Drop your guns!"

The kids crawled off into a corner and were hiding behind a rack of porno magazines.

A voice came from the other side of the rack that Johnny was hiding behind, "You ain't no fucking cops and fuck you if you are anyway."

Shots started blasting through the rack and Johnny tried to slide sideways away from them. After the fourth bullet boomed through the rack, the next shot cut a hole through Johnny's left arm.

Then whoever was firing was squeezing off shots from an empty gun.

"I'm getting the fuck out of here," the same voice yelled.

Despite his arm burning like fire, Johnny jumped to his feet just in time to see a door between two racks of porno magazines swing open and the long stringy haired guy from the liquor store bolted through. Johnny took a shot at him.

*   *   *

The other guy from the van forgot about me the moment that Johnny stood up. He stepped out, raised his pistol, and took careful aim.

At that moment I came out of the video arcade hallway through the curtain. I put the snub nose to his back, squeezed the trigger, and ripped lead through his back bone and heart.

His arm jerked as he died and he blasted a shot that shattered a neon light fixture over Johnny's head.

From behind the counter Ray yelled, "Kill them goddamn-it."

Johnny laughed, and with the hand clutching the .45 he brushed the glass from the neon out of his hair.

"All your boys are dead," he yelled back at Ray.

There was a moment of silence.

The shotgun came sliding out from behind the counter. "That's all I have," Ray shouted. "I'm giving up."

"You come out from behind that counter with both hands in the air," I told Ray. "You even fucking twitch we're gonna shoot you so many times you could model for Swiss cheese."

He stood up slowly with his hands in the air.

"Turn around and put your hands against the wall," Johnny yelled at him pointing his .45 at Ray's head.

He did as he was told.

As soon as he had his hands spread out on the wall, Ray yelled, "Man, my legs are fucking killing me. I got glass stuck in me from my ass to my ankles."

"You think I give a fuck," Johnny yelled back at him.

"I just don't know how long I can stand like this," Ray said.

Johnny came back with, "You start looking like you're gonna slide down that wall I'll help your ass slide all the way down to hell mother-fucker. Don't you even think about moving!"

I went to Johnny and his arm was pumping out blood.

"You gonna be all right?" I asked.

"Fuck no!" He answered. "That's the hand I wipe my ass with. I'll have to make you do that now."

"You'll be all right." I told him.

I grabbed the cell phone out of my pocket and dialed Joe Briggs. He answered on the third ring, almost like he was waiting for this call.

"We're at Ray's Triple X Gallery," I told him. "Bring an ambulance and," I glanced at the kids huddled in the corner, "probably someone from social services."

"What happened out there?" Joe asked.

77

"I ain't got time to talk," I told him. "It ain't pretty and it's still happening. Get out here fast."

I hung up.

"I'm going after the last guy," I told Johnny. "Can you hold out till an ambulance gets here?"

Johnny answered, "Shit, go get him man. I get dizzy from lose of blood, this mother-fucker here is going to die."

CHAPTER 21

I went through the door that the stringy haired guy fled through. Just past that door were wooden stairs leading down into a basement. Of course there was no light on. There never is when I got to go down into this kind of shit.

The stairs went down into pitch blackness. I was getting tired of going down into inky black pits but I never really have a choice.

There was no light switch at the top of the stairs. The wooden steps looked like they lead down into a murky muddy pool of water.

I went down the stairs as quietly as I could. This didn't make any sense at all because anybody down there knew I was coming.

The stairs creaked beneath my feet with every step that I took. This was a deep basement. So deep that the stairs had a bend to the left that plunged me totally into darkness.

Darkness seems to magnify silence.

The light from the shop was a good twenty feet above me when my feet hit the level concrete floor of the basement. I stood at the bottom of the stairs in total blackness crouching, trying to see something in front of me and saw nothing but the strange tracers of light that you see when you close your eyes.

In fact, it was so dark I was kind of wondering if I somehow had closed my eyes on the way down the stairs and blinked to make sure that my eyes were open. Yeah, I had my eyes open. It was just darker than hell down here.

I heard shuffling somewhere in front of me so I stepped to the right in the dark and bumped into a steel support beam.

A scraping sound came from my left.

I wheeled that way with my gun geld out. I wanted to squeeze off a shot but knew that the muzzle flash would give away my exact position.

Something pinged in a distant part of the basement. I crouched low trying to locate the sound with my ears.

Breathing came from my right, like someone sniffling with a runny nose. More shuffling came from my left then a sound like a moan came from behind me.

What the fuck was going on down here? I asked myself. Either this guy can see in the dark and he's just fucking with me or there are more than four guys down here.

Something light brushed my face and I went to wipe it away and it caught in my fingers.

It was a string, a light string.

What the fuck? I thought and pulled it.

A single light bulb came on and illuminated the inside of the section of the basement that I was in.

Lined up and stacked in two layers against the walls of the basement, in the kind of cages you'd see in a dog kennel, were children that I was guessing were between the ages of six and eleven.

They were grimy and dirty and shied away from the light like they hadn't seen much of that for a long time.

There were around twenty kids in these cages and they had the same kind of shell shocked look that I'd seen on the faces of children in Viet Nam whose villages had been bombed to dust.

In the dim bare light of the single bulb I quickly scanned the room and didn't see the stringy haired guy anywhere. What I did see at the far end of the basement was another door leading out.

There was nothing in this room but the kids in their cages. There was nowhere to hide.

Keeping my eyes on the door at the far end, I went to the cage that had a boy in it who looked somewhere around nine. I undid the latch and let him out. He seemed a little less frightened than the others.

"You got to let the rest of them out," I told him.

He nodded.

"Get them out and take them upstairs."

He nodded again and went to work.

I walked to the door at the far end of the basement.

*   *   *

The knob turned and I eased the door open and peered around the edge. The light in this room, again from a single bulb in the ceiling, was on.

I pushed the door all the way open and stepped inside. No one was in the room.

I was alone in here.

It was just me, the camera equipment, a messed up single bed, a couch, and a sturdy wooden chair with leather straps looped around the arms and legs, and a table with the tools on it that had been used to torture and murder the woman I loved.

The room was set up so that beyond the camera equipment was a door. Taped on both sides of the door were dozens of photos. The photos showed the guy still alive upstairs, Ray, and the stringy haired guy, raping the kids from the cages and other kids.

There were other guys in the photos too and also photos of torture. One photo that was of particular importance to me was the one of the stringy haired guy in a black rain coat. He had the mask in his hand that he would put on before he began to torture Sherry.

I went to the door beyond the cameras and eased it open.

It was a corridor.

The corridor was in blackness.

I couldn't step into that hallway with the light shining behind me the way it was. Anyone just beyond my sight would blow me to hell with no problem.

I took aim at the light in the center of the room where Sherry had died and shot it out.

The room was bathed in total blackness.

*   *   *

I stepped out into the inky black corridor.

This time I welcomed the darkness. With this total absence of light if I couldn't see them, they couldn't see me, unless if they had night vision goggles on. I just had to remind myself about that, didn't I?

Moving down the corridor I felt the wall in front of me with my left hand and shuffled forward in a semi-crouch. This corridor was so small if someone started shooting at me being in a crouch probably wouldn't help at all, but what the fuck, it made me feel better.

The tracers of light were back dancing in front of my face like fireflies on acid. That was just my optic nerves searching for something to focus on and finding nothing.

The wall against my left hand was damp and cold. I would have been surprised if it had been any other way. Wintertime around East St. Louis is a cold mother-fucker. This one was colder than most and getting colder all the time.

It was silent down here in the frozen dark. The only sounds I heard were my own breathing, the shuffle of my shoes on the cement floor, and my heart pounding in my chest.

From two rooms over I heard cages being unlocked. The cage doors squeaked as they were swung open and then banged shut a few seconds later.

My foot contacted something and I stumbled and sprawled forward and landed on my elbows and knees on wooden stairs leading upward.

Searching the wall I found a handrail and went up.

The first stair I stepped on creaked beneath my shoe. I held my breath expecting someone to fire down at me in the dark.

After maybe one very long minute, where I heard nothing but the pounding of my own heart in my ears, I took another step up.

This stair didn't make a sound.

The one after it didn't either.

Then I came to a bend in the stairs that mirrored the one leading into the basement back at Ray's. Maybe five or six steps up from the bend I could see a line of light.

That must be the bottom of the door leading in. I crept up the stairs trying to move like a cat.

At the top I stood still and holding my breath I listened.

Silence was all I heard from the other side of the door.

I felt around and found the door handle, turned it, and slowly eased it open.

The question came to me, *Why hadn't he just locked this door behind him?*

I heard a sound like a guitar string being tightened and then a soft ping. Something, an old memory of a sound made me turn, take a running step and dive down the stairs.

The old memory was from Viet Nam. The sound was of a grenade's pin being popped loose.

I slammed into the wall at the bend in the stairs, just as the world behind me exploded in a bright yellow flash that deafened me and knocked me rolling down the rest of the stairs.

I landed on the cement at the bottom of the stairs on my face. My back seemed to be on fire. I rolled over, then a darkness deeper that the blackness already around me, swallowed me up.

PART III

PARTING WORDS

CHAPTER 22

I floated in the darkness between the worlds, gliding weightless in silence. I went nowhere, felt nothing, and the darkness was complete and comforting.

Then, she was there and in my arms, warm and soft I held Sherry to me, and never wanted to let her go.

The silence was all around us.

The darkness was all around us.

We were the only beings in this universe and that was exactly the way I wanted it to be.

I kissed Sherry on the lips and held her, and she whispered to me, "You must go on."

"I want to stay here with you," I told her.

She turned to smoke in my arms but I could still hear her voice. "This place is nowhere," she said. "It is only a meeting place. You must go on. The path you are on now is important."

"I'm going to kill the bastards who took you from me," I shouted.

"Your revenge will be denied for now," Sherry's voice answered. "I was unimportant. You must save the children."

A bright light cut into my eyes, a disk of white light.

I reached for it.

"He's alive!" a voice shouted.

I sat up on the cold cement and wiped dirt out of my hair. Another light appeared beside the first. I could now see it was two cops down here with me.

"Stay down," one of them told me, and put his hand on my shoulder.

I slapped his hand away.

"Get the fuck off me," I told him and stood up.

They shined their flashlights on the stairs I'd just been blown down by the blast of the grenade booby-trap. The way to the next floor was now a tangled mass of splintered wood beams and collapsed cement.

Nobody was going to get through that way.

I retraced my steps with the two cops behind me and went back up into Ray's Triple X Gallery.

An EMT was working on Johnny's arm. The EMT was a sweet looking Mexican woman and Johnny was telling her how much he needed personal nursing. The way his eyes were looking down into the front of her uniform as she bent over applying bandages to his arm, I had a pretty good idea what Johnny wanted to be nursing on.

Later Johnny would ride in the ambulance to the hospital. He did need his arm X-rayed and looked at by a doctor, but he couldn't fool me with all his moaning and groaning. His main reason for wanting to go was so he could keep trying to put the clutch on that cute Mexican EMT.

I can't say I blamed him, either.

The kids were all in a corner of the room with a woman who was trying to get their names from them. She had out a pad and pencil but most of them were too traumatized to even be able to speak.

Joe Briggs had Ray in handcuffs. He motioned for me to come over to where he was.

When I walked over, Ray yelled, "Keep that bastard away from me!"

Joe gave him an open-handed slap to the ear that was hard enough to bust an eardrum. "Shut up!" He told him.

Ray shut up.

"There was another one," I told Joe, "The one that tortured Sherry. He got away."

"I ain't saying shit till I see my lawyer," Ray said.

Me and Joe looked at each other and grinned.

*　　*　　*

Out at the small cinderblock house where I'd left Arnold Jenkins to bleed to death, Ray was only too happy to tell us everything we wanted to know.

The clean-up crew was taking out Jenkin's body as we arrived. They hadn't mopped the blood off the floor yet.

We told them to leave it. Ray got mighty pale when he saw that blood on the floor inside the cage. He told us the name and address of the stringy haired guy.

His name…I can't remember it now. It didn't matter. He was just a thing to me, something that I had to kill. I wrote his address down. It was in West St. Louis County. I put it in my pocket.

The name of the Oriental man who'd cut Sherry's throat, he said, was Tian Kham. He didn't know if he said it right, so I don't know if I wrote it down right.

As I was getting the last name from Ray, a stocky middle-aged under-cover cop came in the door. He had a deeply lined face, a face that looked like he's seen a lot of suffering, and the only way he was going to relieve some of his own pain was to inflict some suffering on someone else.

"That's all I know," Ray said to Joe Briggs. "You can take me to the regular police department now. Tian hired us to grab the woman. I didn't know they were going to hurt her."

That was a lie and we all knew it.

This was when the undercover cop spoke up. "A small blond haired girl," he pulled a photo out of his wallet and shoved it at the bars. "You grabbed her from Wilson Park in Granite City. She was my daughter. Where is she now?"

Ray didn't even look at the photo. "I don't know what you're talking about," he said.

Joe Briggs handed the key to the cage to the undercover cop. "I think you two need to get better acquainted." he told them.

*   *   *

Joe radioed the address of the stringy haired guy and had the building sealed off before we got there.

CHAPTER 23

I followed Joe in my car, and by the time we got to the stringy haired guys apartment, it was getting light outside. The snow was still coming down but the storm never turned into the blizzard it threatened to. The world was covered in a blanket of white, making it look clean and new and innocent.

Too bad the world just wasn't that way.

The stringy haired guy's apartment was in a run-down neighborhood. In the early morning light no one was on the street except for the two police cars out front of his building.

The police lights of the two cruisers were not flashing. This was a situation where the police didn't want to attract very much attention. Joe wanted the extra cops there in case the stringy haired guy tried to run, but he didn't want the media to get wind of this, in case we had to carry this guy away and work on him awhile.

As soon as we got there, Joe got the report from the other cops that no one had entered or left the apartment since they arrived.

It was a ground level apartment. The two of us went to the door.

He knocked.

No answer.

He knocked again.

"This is the police," he said loudly enough for anyone inside to hear him. "Open the door!"

I reached past him and tried the door knob. It was unlocked. The door swung inward and all the way open.

Joe walked in.

I followed.

A TV was turned on. It was tuned to a station that had gone off the air. White noise filled the room.

Joe drew his service revolver.

I drew the snub-nosed .38 I had.

We scanned the room quickly. No one was in the front room or in the dining room that adjoined it.

We went from room to room, checking for anyone hidden. The bathroom was empty. So was his bedroom.

In a second bedroom, that was completely bare of furniture except for a turned over dining room chair against a wall, we found the stringy haired guy.

He was hanging from a light fixture.

The stringy haired guy's face was purple. His eyes were blood shot and were bulging out. His tongue was lolling out of his mouth.

"He probably committed suicide," I told Joe. "He knew I was coming for him."

"Don't flatter yourself," Joe told me. "You're not that scary. He was murdered."

Joe pointed at the chair lying on its side against the wall. "There's no way he kicked that over there. It's too far away from him. Someone made him get up there then jerked the chair out from underneath him."

"Shit!" I said.

"Yeah, that's what we've got now," Joe said. "He came back here and told someone about you and Johnny's raid, and they didn't like it."

I finished for Joe. "So they got the hell out of here and didn't want to leave anyone behind who knew who they were."

"You got it," Joe answered.

"So where are we now?" I asked Joe.

"Only thing we can do is find out who this William Po is. I'd bet anything he knows the man who cut Sherry's throat."

"That's going to be my job," I told Joe.

"Well, if he's in that country you named, Tehan Setar," Joe said, "Then he's a long way outside of my jurisdiction."

"There's one thing I've gotta ask you," I said. "I've always known you to be a by-the-book cop. For this you've been way outside the law. What gives?"

Joe smiled. It was the kind of smile that would make a criminal in a jail cell shit down both legs if he saw his jailer smiling like that.

"The laws were written to govern mankind. I am a by-the-book cop when I'm dealing with the human race. These things," he pointed at the hanging stringy haired guy, "are freaks of nature. They need to be removed from the world however it can be done. They don't deserve the protection of the law. They sure won't get it from me."

"What are we going to do with him?" I asked.

Joe said, "I'll send the uniforms home then I'll go through the place looking for names. I don't expect to find anything. Then I'll seal it up. Somebody will find him in a few weeks when he gets really ripe."

CHAPTER 24

There was nothing more that I could do for now and it had been one very long night. I drove home and wondered about what Sherry told me.

I hadn't told anyone about that.

I had thought that seeing Sherry, when I was knocked into that strange half dream state by the grenade blast, was just a type of wish fulfillment dream. I wanted to see her, so I did.

Now, I wasn't so sure.

Sherry told me that, for now, I would be denied my revenge. That couldn't be truer. I wanted to be the one to snuff out that stringy haired guy's life but someone else beat me to it.

That was downright prophetic.

There's no way I could have known in advance that we'd be finding that guy already dead, so my unconscious mind didn't dream Sherry's message up.

About the other part of Sherry's message, "Save the children!" I didn't have a clue what that meant. Yeah, I know I'd gotten those kids out of that basement but something inside me told me she wasn't talking about them.

There was something bigger going on here that I didn't know about.

Only time, and a lot more bloodshed, would reveal those secrets.

*   *   *

After taking a shower and catching some sleep I went by and checked on Johnny. They just patched his arm up, took some X-rays, and sent him home. The bullet he took in the arm passed clean on through and didn't even touch a bone or a major artery. The arm would be sore as hell for a few weeks but it was nothing serious.

Johnny did manage to get the name and phone number from that cute Mexican EMT. Her name was Lola Martinez.

"You know how it is," Johnny told me. "Whatever Lola wants, Lola gets, as long as what she wants involves me feeding her my prime pork sausage."

One thing's for sure, Johnny would never change.

After I left Johnny's I ate a few burgers and some onion rings at a Burger King then headed back home.

Sleeping that night was not easy. I wasn't exhausted so I didn't just fall out like I'd done that morning. No matter how I lay in my bed, the bed seemed far too big for just one person.

I had the need to reach out and touch my woman, to feel her beside me. But she was no longer there.

Having Tom sleep beside me just didn't do the trick either. Around two in the morning I ended up back on the couch and fell asleep with the TV playing some old monster movie.

If the monsters I met in my dreams were no worse than the one's in the movie then I'd be able to rest easy. The problem was the monsters on my mind were from the real world, and I couldn't do away with them by just turning a flip of the switch.

CHAPTER 25

In the morning I cleaned up as much as I could, put on my best set of clothes, and went to Sherry's funeral.

Before I left I took a good look in the mirror and realized that I looked like warmed over death. To hell with it, I thought. Today I wasn't making an appearance in anybody's fashion show. They could take me as I am or just get the fuck out of my way.

*   *   *

The funeral was a grim affair.

Aren't they all?

All the guys were dressed in suits and ties. All the women were dressed in their finest dresses. After a preacher said a few words, not a one of which I can recall, all the people filed past Sherry in her casket.

It all seemed ludicrous to me.

I forced myself to go and take a look at Sherry in that box. The mortician had done a good job, maybe too good, or maybe just good enough.

It didn't look like Sherry laying there. The thing in the casket looked like a wax replica of Sherry done from a photograph.

*   *   *

At the cemetery the priest was saying some more words before they lowered Sherry into the ground, and all that was going through my head was, *Why the fuck can't you just get this done? Just get it over with. That's not the woman I love in that box. Don't you understand that?*

The preacher kept droning on.

Tension was building inside me. My head was getting hot. I felt like busting somebody upside the head, and the priest, who, if Sherry wasn't dead already, would've bored her to death, was the only person I was seeing.

Johnny was at my side. He looked in my face.

"Come on," he said, and dragged me away before I did something that would have been very fucking ignorant.

We walked off to the side and Jeanette came up beside us.

"I'm going to miss her," I told them.

"I know Bro," Johnny said, and as Jeanette held me I cried.

PART IV

TRAVEL PLANS

CHAPTER 26

The phone rang, and before I knew what I was doing, I had it in my hand.

"John Dark," I said. My words were probably slurred because a bottle of Jack Daniels helped me sleep last night. I wasn't used to the mornings after a drunk anymore, and the pain in my head was epic.

The night before was just a blur.

"It's Nash Graham," the voice on the other end came back. "I need to meet you somewhere as soon as you can get your ass in gear."

"Any word about who William Po is?" I asked.

"Like I said," he repeated, "I need to meet with you."

"Give me a half hour," I told Nash. "Be in the parking lot of Patty's Kitten House."

He hung up.

* * *

It was a few minutes after 11 AM when I arrived at Patty's Kitten House, pulled through the gate, and drove into the parking lot. Nash Graham was already parked in a space near the far fence of the lot.

I pulled up beside him and got out.

He waved me around to his driver's side door, so I walked around and got in.

It's never ceased to amaze me how much Graham looks like your average middle-aged high school principle, when in actuality he's one of the most heartless bastards that I've ever met. You don't get to be the head of the DEA in the Midwest without being ruthless in the extreme.

To be a good hunter you have to be deadlier and cleverer than your prey. Nash Graham's prey was the large drug dealers and traffickers in the Midwest. When he targeted one to take down it wasn't even a contest.

I slid in beside Graham. "Did you find out who William Po is?" I asked.

He laughed under his breath. "You come right to the point don't you," Graham said.

"Ain't either one of us here for socializing," I told him.

"No, we're not," he agreed. "All right, this is what I've got. There's a little country in Southeast Asia, about the size of Delaware, on the border that separates Laos and Thailand. It's something like a principality. The country's name is Tehan Setar.

"William Po is the name of the leader of a group of rebels that have been ambushing that country's soldiers and blowing up things for years. They've been calling themselves freedom fighters.

"What the hell this could have to do with your girlfriend's murder I don't have any idea. But I do know that just my few inquiries got somebody mighty pissed off in our government.

"I went through official channels to get my info, and a direct order was sent down from the state department that I was to cease all inquiries in this region or I'd find myself unemployed."

He saw my eyebrows rise.

"Yeah, it surprised the hell out of me, too," Graham said. "Someone with enough clout to even think about having me fired has to be extremely high up in the government.

"I don't like being threatened. I did some checking through some sources that can't be traced. The man who tried to warn me off is a Senator named Jack Craven. He's one of those holier than thou bastards who are always trying to push religious right based legislation through The House.

"He shouldn't have any interest in a place like Tehan Setar, or anything that goes on over there. But he sure took interest in me when I asked a few questions.

"There's something else," Graham continued. "That country's economics just don't seem to add up. The only exports appear to be poppies and marijuana, and there's far more money coming out of that country than there appears to be going in. This equation does not balance."

I told Graham, "Looks like I'm going to have to take a trip to the Orient myself. I'm going to need to speak to this William Po."

"The Tehan Setar military has been hunting him for years. They haven't caught him yet," Graham said, "Happy hunting."

*   *   *

As Graham drove out of the parking lot, it occurred to me that I was going to be needing quite a bit of money if I was going to be traveling to Tehan Setar to track down the man who murdered Sherry. Plane tickets and hotel arrangements in obscure Oriental nations I'm sure don't come cheap.

I had a little bit of money in the bank but not enough to even consider funding this trip.

My eyes settled on the Porsche Sherry gave me as a gift. It sat in the far corner of the parking lot covered by a blanket of snow.

I knew what I had to do.

*   *   *

Patty's Kitten House was open for business–as–usual but the mood inside was very subdued. The DJ was playing slow songs and the girls on the stages were taking their clothes off in slow motion for the few customers in the place. No one complained about that.

Slow motion is a good speed for taking a good long look.

I'd left Ron Martin in charge and he was behind the bar getting somebody a beer when I walked in. He gave me a friendly wave and I waved back.

I went to the DJ and told him I'd need his mike for a few minutes. He got up and headed for the bar to refresh his own drink.

I sat in the DJ's chair, took the mike in my hand, and pressed the button. A squelch of feedback came from the speakers for a moment. When it died down I spoke.

"This is John Dark," I announced. "I'm the owner of the black Porsche in the corner of the parking lot. It's now for sale for thirty thousand dollars. That Porsche runs like a striped assed ape and it's worth a lot more than thirty thousand but I need the money. I'll be hanging around for a little while so if you're interested see me at the bar."

I gave the chair back to the DJ and took a stool at the bar.

As soon as I sat down Ron Martin was beside me. "Man if you need money all you need to do is say so," he told me.

"I need more than just a friendly loan," I told him.

"This is about finding Sherry's killer, ain't it?" Ron told me.

"Yeah," I answered. "I gotta leave the country for a while."

"I need to talk to you about something," Ron said and motioned for me to follow him.

I followed Ron through a door behind one of the stages to Sherry's office. When we were inside he closed the door behind us.

He went and sat on the chair behind the desk and said, "Sherry was kind of like a sister to me man, or maybe in a way she was something like a mother. After I busted my leg and was out of the NFL I had more money than I knew what to do with. Hell, I still do. But I was kind of drifting. I didn't know what to do with myself. Sherry was more than just a boss. A lot of times, we just talked. Actually I was the one that talked. She just listened.

"When I needed it she was there for me. When I found out that I liked men as well as women she was the one that told me it was all right, that I wasn't less of a man, that I was just who I was and no different than I had always been.

"I don't know what I would have done if she hadn't been there for me. If you know who killed Sherry then I'm going to help put them in the ground. I'm not going to take no for an answer either."

I knew Ron was serious so I told him everything that had happened so far.

When I was done, Ron told me, "Get ready to pack some bags brother. We're going to the Far East to bust some heads until we get some satisfaction. I'm funding this whole damn hunting party."

"Are you sure you can afford this," I asked him.

"Shit," Ron answered with a grin. "The NFL paid me real good and I invested well. I got enough money for three lifetimes. Besides, at heart I'm just a big dumb country-boy. Heaven for me is a double-wide trailer, a big screen TV, a hot sex partner, and an icebox full of beer. I already got those covered."

This was going to be an interesting trip.

CHAPTER 27

After we talked over what we had to take care of before we left, Ron called Lambert Airport and got us two tickets, leaving for Bangkok the next day at noon. When Ron got through with that call he phoned Candi Divine to let her know he was going to be gone for a while.

The voice coming from the other end of the phone line was loud enough for me to clearly hear, "What! You ain't going nowhere without me!"

Ron's conversation with Candi after that was short and to the point. After a few, "yes dears," he was back on the phone calling the airline for another plane ticket.

*   *   *

I went to my apartment building and stopped by Rosa Delgado's place. When Rosa answered the door her face lit up then went dark almost immediately.

"I'm so sorry about Sherry," Rosa said, and gave me a strong hug.

"I can't talk about Sherry or I'll end up losing it," I told Rosa.

"Sure, I understand," Rosa said.

Rosa was a chunky middle-aged Mexican woman who I used to pay to clean my apartment once a week when I lived here before. She was a good friend, more like family than just somebody I knew.

You might think that someone as poor as me would never hire someone to clean their place. Just chalk it up to me being a lazy white boy. I'd rather pay somebody else to do it than do it myself whether I really had enough money to afford it or not.

"I got to leave town for a while," I told Rosa. "Can you keep an eye on Tom while I'm gone?"

"Sure," Rosa answered. "I still got the key from when you were here before. Rodney never changes any locks. If we want to do it, he don't care. But he never does."

"If you can, just make sure he's fed and watered and drop his turds on the assholes that sleep in the alley below the window," I told her.

"I can do that," Rosa said. "I'll leave the window open too. Tom's like you. He likes to come and go as he wants."

"That he does," I said.

"Do you know when you'll be back?" Rosa asked.

"Not exactly," I said.

"You'll never change," Rosa said. "But I wouldn't want you to. It'd be like gelding a bull."

"That'd be painful," I told her.

*   *   *

I walked over to Johnny's Bar and Grill. He had his left arm in a sling and was telling a drunk he'd slap him silly with his one good arm if he didn't shut the fuck up and get the hell out of his tavern.

Johnny always did practice good customer relations.

I sat on a bar stool and Johnny got me a Michelob on draft. He set it in front of me.

"Did you just hit the lottery?" I asked him.

His look said, "What?"

"A while back you wouldn't give me anything but that shit tasting Schlitz. Now you're giving me the good stuff even before I ask for it. What gives?"

He grabbed the glass up and took a big swallow out of it.

"Fuck-it! I'll drink it myself," he said. Then he downed the entire glass.

"Hey, I wanted that," I told Johnny.

"I wanted it, too," he said and got me another one.

"I'm leaving town," I said.

"Figured you would," he answered.

I filled Johnny in on heading to Tehan Setar with Ron Martin and Candi Divine.

Johnny said, "That's going to be like a goddamn traveling freak show."

"You can tell Ron that yourself," I told him.

"Shit!" Johnny said. "That big mother-fucker! I may be stupid but I'm not that goddamned stupid."

We drank for a few hours, told some jokes back and forth, and watched some really bad TV. Sometime during the night Johnny asked me to give him Graham's number.

I gave it to him and asked, "What do you want him for? I didn't know you did any business that would have anything to do with what he's into."

"There are lots of goddamned things you don't know," Johnny said. "I just got a bone to pick with him. It ain't nothing for you to worry about."

"Well, fuck it then," I told him.

Around midnight I headed home.

My small run-down apartment seemed too large and empty without Sherry there with me. Any room seemed too large without her in it.

I was going to have to get used to that.

BOOK TWO

PART I

INTO THE EAST

CHAPTER 28

The city Bangkok, Thailand; exotic, mysterious, and at first glance, to me it looked a hell of a lot like any China Town in any major US city. The main difference was that this China Town wasn't just a neighborhood. This China Town went on and on. It was big.

Ron Martin, Candi Divine, and me got off the flight in Bangkok, grabbed our bags, grabbed a taxi, and went directly to a hotel. We'd just taken a long flight and I was bushed.

One thing did happen to remind me of where the hell we were. The three of us about shit a brick when the taxi driver pulled out into traffic and went the wrong way down the fucking road. After we yelled a few times at him, "What the hell do you think you're doing?" And him laughing at us, we realized everybody was driving on the wrong side of the road.

Well, the wrong side over here turns out to be the right side. Welcome to fucking Thailand.

Where Candi and Ron spent the flight in two seats side by side cuddling and cat napping, I spent the flight staring out the window trying to make plans for who we were going to see, and how we were going to track down William Po.

If anyone could point me in the direction of Sherry's killer it would have to be William Po.

Sherry had been sending him large amounts of money. Why? I'd find that out when I found him. Sherry's killers asked her over and over again, "Where is William Po?"

Someone wanted William Po bad enough to kill an innocent woman just to get information of his whereabouts. William Po had made dangerous enemies and now they made me theirs.

Our starting place would have to be someone who was friendly to us and who knew the local area. Since none of us knew anyone in Tehan Setar I brought the name and address of the one person in that country that was in Sherry's address book.

Sister Mary Sheridon was the first person we had to talk to. After that, who the hell knew?

*   *   *

After I caught a few hours of sleep I met Ron and Candi in the hotel's restaurant.

Candi came in wearing some casual slacks and a nicely styled loose blouse. The blouse hid the bulges of muscle on Candi's arms and shoulders and did nothing to hide the bulges of her breasts. She looked all woman, even if it was in an overstated way.

I'd only seen Candi at the clubs where she never had hardly any clothes on at all, and on the flight over here she wore tight jeans and a tee shirt exposing arms that were frightening.

Candi noticed my eyes wander over her and she beamed a large toothy smile.

Ron noticed and laughed.

"See John," Candi told me. "I can be a lady when I want to be."

I said, "Yeah, the girl with something extra for sure."

They both laughed and Ron leaned over and kissed Candi a big wet smacker.

"Y'all are fucking crazy," I told them.

That made them laugh harder.

The restaurant's menus were the kind that had pictures of the dishes as well as written descriptions of what the dishes were.

I was glad they had the pictures because I didn't know what the hell the words said.

Even when I was in the Special Forces as a Search and Destroy Specialist in Viet Nam, I didn't learn very much of the local language and what little I knew was long forgotten.

The only words I learned in Viet Nam were the ones that had to do with me getting food beer and women. Making someone understand that I wanted food or beer was harder for me to do than making a woman understand that I wanted to do the horizontal tango.

For food and beer I'd point at my mouth and make eating or drinking motions. A lot of the time people looked at me like I was a fucking idiot.

To get a woman I'd just grab my dick and hold up some money. It was funny how they always understood what the hell that meant.

We were in Thailand now so even if I had been fluent in Viet Namese I doubt I would have understood the language spoken here anyway.

Ron and Candi ordered some noodle dishes. I didn't want to take any chances not knowing exactly what I was ordering and got a large bowl of chicken fried rice. With my luck if I ordered a noodle dish I'd find out later that I'd just chewed up an expensive bowl of Earth worms.

As Candi was slurping down a forkful of noodles Ron asked me, "So what's the first move you figure we ought to make here?"

"Well," I told them. "I don't know about you but I 'm feeling mighty naked without a weapon. Inside the city it seems about as safe as St. Louis, but out in the country I can tell you from experience there's some crazy mother-fuckers out there."

Candi asked, "What are we going to do about the border crossing? I doubt they're going to let us carry arms from Thailand into Tehan Setar."

"We're going to make our crossing through the jungle where we won't have to worry about that. We're going into that country with every intention of tracking down and killing one of their citizens. We don't want to leave any trace that we were there at all."

* * *

Night was falling in Bangkok as we left the hotel to go gun hunting.

I told Ron I'd go by myself and get the three of us some hand guns. He wouldn't have any of that, saying, "No way man. We came over here to do a job together. Besides, I'm footing this bill. I want to know what kind of fire power I'm buying before I have to stake my life on it."

Ron told Candi we'd be back in a little while.

"Yeah, we all gonna be back in a little while," Candi told him. "I ain't letting you boys go off and chase no Asian poon tang."

"Babe, you know we ain't gonna do that," Ron told her.

"Damn right I know that," Candi told him. Cause I'm gonna be right there."

"Fuck-it," I told the two of them. "Why don't we just invite the entire fucking hotel and make it a goddamn parade."

CHAPTER 29

We had a taxi take us to a street market. I figured that was as good a place as any to start.

The weather was hot. I'm not exactly sure of the temperature but after leaving snow in St. Louis I was sweating my balls off in this steamy son-of-a-bitch.

People were still out in droves. Around here, this street market was a twenty four hour thing. We strolled through the market taking in everything that was around us, getting ourselves accustomed to where we were.

There was a sea of faces all around us. Most of the faces were Asian and in the dark almond shaped eyes, black hair and coffee with lots of cream skin I saw Sherry everywhere. There's no way I could live over here permanently, not with so many people around me who would remind me that the woman I loved was dead.

If I lived the rest of my life in this place it would be like living in a nation of ghosts.

The smells of exotic spicy food being sold by street vendors engulfed us. Some of the spices were so hot just sniffing the breeze made your eyes water. Kids came up begging for coins. Most of them knew a word or two of English. They sure knew more of my language than I knew of theirs. We didn't give them anything. If you ever give one of them anything you'll never be able to get rid of the rest of the pack.

After they followed us through all kinds of open-aired street shops for about fifteen minutes they gave up and went off in search of other tourists to beg from.

Everything was on display out in that open-air street market. Leather goods, computers, cell phones, electronics, you name it, it was for sale.

We were looking for guns.

Because we weren't the only tourists roaming around here, and we were ease dropping in on the conversations around us, we could tell that most of the people running these make shift mini-stores had a working knowledge of

English. That was why, when we came to a dealer of knives and swords, I told the guy right up front that I was looking for weapons that were for more than just being on display.

"I do not know what you mean," the man told me as he showed me the keen edge of a Samurai Sword priced at fifty dollars. His smile and the look in his eyes told me he knew exactly what I was talking about.

The four of us were alone in his small shop that was only made up of three cloth walls and a cloth ceiling. I looked at Ron and he stepped forward so that his bulk blocked the view of anyone outside.

"We'll pay well for guns," I told the man, and Ron dug into his pocket and showed the shop owner a roll of bills, while Candi kept a look-out for anyone taking notice outside.

The man's eyes sparkled when he saw the money.

"I do not sell that product myself," he said. "For a price I can take you to someone who does. It is not far. I can take you there."

"All right," I told the man. "But we don't pay you until we see the guns. We see the guns we'll pay you. You go on your merry way. Deal?"

"Yes," the shop owner said.

The shop owner said something in Thai then and I just shook my head at him asking, "What was that?"

"Sorry," he answered quickly. "I forgot myself for a moment. I was just asking if you are sure you do not need some of my blades. They are the best quality in all of Asia."

"We might come back for a few tomorrow," I told him. "Tonight we need to get what we came for."

"Of course," he answered.

He then pulled back a fold of the cloth and yelled something in Thai to someone outside his tent. A moment later a ragged looking old man with rotting teeth came through the cloth doorway.

They exchanged words. The wrinkled old dude looked at us and sighed, then pulled up a stool and sat down next to a display of swords and knives.

"We go now," the shop owner said, and lead us out into the street.

* * *

We followed the shop owner through the street market, then onto some dimly lit side streets.

The route he took us on was through narrow walkways. The pavement felt like cobblestones and the air smelt of urine and garbage. We were moving farther into one of the poorest sections of Bangkok, places where the police didn't dare come.

If the police were chasing a criminal and he ran into this neighborhood they'd break that chase off. Here they were outnumbered ten to one. That's not good odds for anybody.

Ron noticed that Candi was lagging back from us as we traveled into the Bangkok ghetto.

"Hey darlin'... get on up here with us," he told her. "I don't want anyone jumping out of the dark and grabbing my baby."

"I am the woman," Candi said. "And here I must walk behind my man." Candi's voice was soft and she actually sounded kind of meek. Candi just wasn't like that. I was wondering what the hell was up myself.

"What the fuck are you talking about?" Ron asked.

"In this land I must bow to the will of my man," Candi said.

"Shit," Ron said. "I'll test that one back at the hotel. Get on up here with us."

"Your woman has realized her rightful place," the shop owner said. "That is good."

That is really fucking strange, is what I was thinking.

CHAPTER 30

We walked about what I estimate was a half mile into this extreme ghetto, passing moaning drunks laying in gutters full of their own piss and shit, dope dealers selling their drugs to ragged street people, and scabby looking prostitutes that radiated disease and filth, when the shop owner took us down a long narrow alley with tall brick walls on both sides.

The alley ended in a dead end with a door in its center. The shop owner pressed a button and an intercom spoke to him some garbled words.

He answered back in Thai and the door buzzed.

The shop owner pushed the door open and stepped through.

Ron and me stepped inside. Candi came in after us and stepped to the side behind the shop owner.

This room was like the gun section of a good sized pawn shop. On the walls were all kinds of rifles and shotguns. In a glass display case directly in front of us was a good selection of some deadly looking hand guns.

Behind the counter stood two young Thai's, both wore wicked looking smiles. One reached under the counter.

Candi grabbed the shop owner by the hair of the head and jerked him backward against her. A knife flashed in her hand and she pressed the blade of what looked like a miniature Samurai Sword to the shop owner's throat.

"Father!" One of the Thai's behind the counter gasped involuntarily reaching forward. The family resemblance between the two Thais and the shop owner was obvious. This business of weapons sales was a family business. The Thais behind the counter were the shop owner's sons.

"Don't even flinch," Candi growled at them. Then she spoke to them in their own language which surprised the hell out Ron and me.

The Thais froze.

Candi told me and Ron, "I barely understood this asshole telling the old man he was going to rip us off, but I understood the old fuck loud and clear when he said to gut us so they could sell our innards to the cat food plant. I like cats as much as anyone but I don't feel like being dinner for them."

"It was just a joke," the shop owner said. "We talk like that. We were just joking."

"Yeah," Ron said, "Well the jokes on you now, ain't it?"

"We'll kill you," one of the young Thais said.

"And your father will die," I told them.

"You need guns, OK, OK!" The shop owner said. "We sell you guns. Good guns. Good price."

"Damn right you will," I told him.

"You boys slowly put your hands on the counter," Ron told the two young Thais.

The young guys looked at their father who nodded.

"We will do the deal the right way tonight," he told them.

I went behind the counter and got a shiny .38 and a box of shells. I quickly loaded it.

Ron was checking out three assault rifles on a wall rack. "What the fuck are these?" He asked.

One of the Thais answered. "AKS-74U submachine guns, black market assault rifles, very good weapons."

Ron plucked one of the submachine guns off the wall and held it out in one hand, testing its weight. He liked what he felt. He dry-fired it and broke it down then put it back together real fast. There was a pile of old army duffle bags in the corner. Ron took one and put the three AKS-74Us in it and grabbed about ten boxes of shells and dropped them in.

"Those babies are light," Ron told us. "Why I even think my honey could handle one of them."

"I can handle anything that you can, darling," Candi told Ron.

I tossed a .38 to Ron and a box of bullets. He loaded it quickly.

Ron kept his eyes on the two Thais and his finger on the trigger as Candi lowered the knife from the shop owner's throat, went behind the counter, selected a chrome-plated .45, got some shells, and loaded it.

When she came back from behind the counter we motioned the shop owner over next to his sons with our pistols.

We backed toward the door with Ron carrying the loaded duffle bag over his shoulder.

The shop owner and his two sons looked at us over the counter. "I suppose you are going to kill us now," the shop owner said.

"That wouldn't be a bad idea," I answered him. "But we might be back this way."

Ron dug into his pocket and came out with a roll of bills. "There's two thousand there," Ron said. "That should more than cover what we got."

He tossed the bills to the shop owner.

"Don't follow us," I told them and we left.

*　　*　　*

We backed out of the alley, expecting at any moment for the door to fly open and someone to start spraying bullets at us.

It never happened.

We walked through the narrow streets in the general direction we came from until we came to a wide open street that cars actually drove on and where businesses besides strip clubs and bars were open. We'd passed the border of the extreme ghetto and were back among the land of the living.

Taxis were driving by; we flagged one down and gave him the address of our hotel.

On the way, Ron asked Candi, "Where'd you learn how to speak this slop-chewy stuff anyway?"

"I had a roommate in Chicago. She taught me some. I actually forgot I knew it until those two guys started talking and I recognized some of the words."

"Did she teach you some of them Oriental sex techniques?" Ron asked.

"We weren't that close," Candi told him.

"Yeah," Ron said. "Well, since we are in this here territory you are going to follow me around and do everything I say, right?"

"Sure thing," Candi answered. "Right after hell freezes over."

CHAPTER 31

That night in the hotel room we thoroughly inspected our new toys. All three of our pistols checked out perfectly. Mine was as good as any I'd ever bought back in the states.

The AKS-74U's, they were some downright sweet assault weapons. This was a rifle that actually folded up the stock to its side so that it became only about three feet long, small enough to fit in a suit case. The clips were big. They held thirty rounds. Ron had filled up the entire bottom of the duffle bags with loaded clips.

We were set.

That guy who cut Sherry's throat had better be praying and giving his heart to god, because we were coming after him, and his ass belonged to me.

* * *

In the morning, we rented a Subaru and Ron paid for our rooms the next month in advance. We figured if we weren't done with what we had to do, and back here laying over and waiting for a plane within a month, then things had went wrong and we'd more than likely be dead.

We bought a roadmap that covered the countries of Thailand, Tehan Setar, and Laos and stocked up on some camping gear and bought a couple extra changes of camouflage clothes. We didn't know if we were going to need this stuff but it wouldn't hurt having it if we did.

Then, we headed out of town.

CHAPTER 32

Did I say already that it is hot in South East Asia? If I didn't, well I tell you what, it was hotter than sitting buck naked in a big ass frying pan.

The air conditioning in the Subaru quit five minutes outside of Bangkok. In ten minutes we were cooking. Opening the windows made it worse. We were sticky, sweaty and miserable. The humidity was extremely high. It must have been somewhere around a hundred and fifty percent. I felt like I was swimming in my clothes and the water was really rank.

Our clothes stuck to us like wet tissue paper. That was one of the few good things because with Candi's monster sized tits, with her shirt stuck to her, she was a sight to behold. Made me think that god has got to have one hell of a bad sense of humor to put a dick and balls between that woman's legs.

Yeah, Candi was the girl with something extra. It was mind boggling.

Everything out in the countryside was green and bright. Bright really isn't the right word for it. The sun was blinding.

I left Bangkok driving on a four lane highway. Pretty soon that dwindled down to a two lane road.

The border of Tehan Setar was one hundred and fifty miles from Bangkok, so about seventy miles out, I turned off onto a smaller road, the kind we would call a county road in the states, and followed that north for a few hours.

The smaller road quickly turned into a dirt road with large pot holes, where we had to pass a lot of ox and mule drawn wagons carrying all kinds of stuff.

The going got slow, real slow. We maybe averaged five miles an hour.

I made a few more turns onto roads that I thought would lead us in the general direction of Tehan Setar, when I realized that to be heading in the direction that I thought we should be going, the sun was on the wrong side of the car.

I told this to Ron and Candi and we all started trying to read road signs to figure out where the hell we were in relation to our map.

The problem was there weren't too many signs and what few there were, were only in Thai. And even though Candi knew quite a few spoken Thai words, none of us read Thai.

We were fucking lost.

"Man, why didn't you buy a goddamned compass?" Ron asked me.

"Yeah, right," I told him. "Like we'd just head west until we hit the East coast of the U.S., right?"

"Actually, if you head directly East from here you'll probably hit Mexico," Candi told us.

She was wrong too, so I just told her, "Thanks for the fucking geography lesson. That really helps."

"I knew you needed it," she told me.

We came around a bend in the road then, bouncing over pot holes hard enough to knock fillings loose. In the distance the road ran through a cluster of short squat houses. Made of mortared together stones with thatched roofs the houses were more like huts than anything else.

"I'm going to pull in there," I told Ron and Candi. "I gotta figure out where the fuck we are."

When we got closer to the huts I could see that this was a small town of about fifty or sixty of those small dwellings. There were a few wood buildings among the huts that looked like businesses of some sort.

One of the businesses looked like it might be a restaurant. It wasn't Red Lobster, that's for sure, but there were tables and people were sitting and eating inside.

I parked in front and we went in.

The people inside were greasy and sweaty and smelled to high heaven. Hard working people were sitting around tables downing beers and eating spicy food.

We went and sat at a table.

A skinny old grey haired woman came up to the table.

"I'll take a Cervesa," Ron told the woman.

"We ain't in Mexico, dumb-ass," I told Ron.

"I don't give a fuck," Ron said. "I need a fucking beer."

Candi said something to the old woman.

She laughed and answered while pointing at the two of us.

When she went away Ron asked Candi what that was about.

Candi said, "I ordered us a round of beers and she told me the two of you remind her of Laurel and Hardy."

"Fuck that old bitch," Ron said.

*　*　*

The beers tasted good.

Either that or we were so hot and thirsty stagnant piss would have tasted good.

The first beers went down fast.

When the old woman came back Candi asked for directions to the Tehan Setar border. The old woman told Candi that she never left the town and didn't know the way, but we could get directions from the supplies store next door. We got three beers for the road.

With beers in hand we headed to the supply store.

The dusty street was quiet except for the sounds of bird calls coming from trees beyond the cluster of huts.

The supplies store was really just an Oriental version of an old fashioned General Store. It had everything in it that the local people needed.

An attractive Asian woman in a blouse and blue jeans was stocking the shelves when we entered. Unless I say otherwise, everybody I mention in Asia was Asian. That makes sense, doesn't it?

Candi went to the woman and in her own language asked her for directions to the Tehan Setar border.

Smiling politely the woman asked her in English, "Why is it you wish to go to Tehan Setar?"

Candi glanced at us then answered quickly, "We're just tourists that got lost in your beautiful countryside."

The woman's polite smile vanished. She gave Candi, then the two of us, a mean look then said, "There are no tourists that go to Tehan Setar, only western devils who come to rape our children. I will not help you. Leave my store!" She pointed at the door as though we'd forgotten where it was.

"Hey lady," I started, "I don't know what..."

"Leave now!" She screamed at us. "You are not welcome here. Get out!"

Well, we'd worn out our welcome in there so we left. I didn't know what the hell had gotten into her but we weren't getting any directions.

Out in the street, about fifty yards from our Subaru, there was a commotion going on.

We crossed the street to our car as three guys in military fatigues, dressed like soldiers, dragged two kids, a little boy and a girl, from one of the huts toward a pick-up truck that had some other kids in the back end. The kids in the truck looked like they were chained together.

A man and a woman were yelling curses at the soldiers.

We got in our car and I reached under the seat and got the .38 I'd stashed there. Ron pulled his .38 out, and Candi dug her .45 out of her industrial sized hand bag she'd bought before leaving the airport in St. Louis.

All three of us had the same thing in our heads. This looked like it was going to get ugly.

Candi whispered over the seat to Ron and me, "They're stealing their children to sell them in Tehan Setar. The man and woman are begging them not to."

Words echoed in my head, words spoken to me by a dead woman. "You must save the children," Sherry had said to me.

A soldier backhanded the father with the butt of a pistol, knocking him to the dirt. He was the only one of the three with a weapon in his hands. The other two were busy trying to keep control of the kids.

The woman screamed and the same soldier punched her, knocking her from her feet.

"We're taking these sons-of-bitches out," I told Ron and Candi, and drove the Subaru toward the soldiers.

I drove slowly and turned like I was going around the disturbance. When we were directly across from the soldiers I yelled, "Hey!"

All the soldiers simultaneously stopped and looked at me in the car. I shoved the .38 out the window and pumped three shots onto the armed soldier's chest.

Hell, I'd come all the way to South East Asia to do an old fashioned Los Angeles drive-by shooting.

Ron and Candi barreled out of their car doors.

Candi grabbed the soldier that was dragging the little girl by the hair of his head, and jerked an entire handful loose while punching him in the face with her left fist.

The soldier staggered backward and went down on his ass.

"Ain't your momma never taught you how to play with girls?" Candi yelled at him, and kicked him in the teeth.

When the other soldier saw the locomotive that was Ron Martin coming at him, he let go of the boy and tried to run. He only got three steps before Ron clubbed him in the side of the head with his ham of a fist, and knocked him sprawling face first in the dirt.

People who had been hiding in the huts came out now.

The soldiers were down and out but that didn't stop the crowd of sixty or seventy people from the village from taking their revenge.

They grabbed whatever they could get their hands on: sticks, hammers, knives, shovels, eating forks, anything and attacked the three soldiers.

It wasn't pretty what they did to those guys in the fatigue uniforms but I can't say they didn't have it coming. When the vengeful villagers were done clubbing and stabbing, those three boys looked like seasoned hamburger meat dressed in bloody rags.

CHAPTER 33

When that orgy of slaughter was over the woman from the General Store came to us and apologized saying, "I am so sorry for how I acted toward you. It is a terrible thing. Bandits steal our children and sell them to Tehan Setar, where wealthy westerners pay large amounts of money to be allowed to rape them. Our government will not protect us. We are alone out here."

I told her our names and the real reason we were in the country, and why I had to get into Tehan Setar. I'd already killed somebody here. Her knowing I intended on killing somebody else couldn't hurt very much.

When I was done, she told us, "I am Mai Lin Wu. I will take you to the border where there are no guards and wish you good luck. The man who killed your woman is probably one of those who do this evil to my people. If there were no buyers, there would be no reason for the bandits to take our children. They are the only thing of value that we have."

The crowd around the three bodies was thinning out. With their rage temporarily spent, most of the villagers had simply gone home. A few of the men were going through the bandit's pockets and were collecting the weapons from inside the truck. Another man got the keys for the chains and was releasing the children.

"What are you going to do with the bodies?" I asked Mai Lin, indicating what was left of the three bandits.

She turned and said something in Thai to the man who was releasing the children. He answered her back immediately.

Mai Lin said, "They will bury them in the jungle, return the children to their homes, then sell the truck for cash a long way from here. If the police ever find the bodies they would not care anyway. These bandits are like non-people in our country. Officially, they do not exist."

"That's good," Ron told her. "I'd hate to think we just dogged somebody important."

"Their kind is important," Mai Lin told us, "Because of the misery they cause."

*   *   *

When everyone calmed down and the bodies had been dragged away, Mai Lin locked up her store and invited us to her home to have a meal before we set out again on the road.

I got to admit, after this morning, a home cooked lunch sounded good.

Mai Lin's home was virtually identical to the rest of the homes in her village, just a small hut with no electricity or running water.

Despite this, the dwelling was clean and uncluttered, the few pieces of furniture and decorations that Mai Lin had, seemed to fit together just right to create a harmonious environment. This was one woman who definitely knew the meaning of Feng Shui.

Feng Shui was something that Sherry told me about. I pretty much just figured it to be a load of bullshit, until I walked into this woman's home.

This home was small, the furnishings were few and simple, but the way everything was arranged created an overall effect that was soothing to the senses.

This place was Feng Shui in action.

Would I use this when I got back in East St. Louis to create a more harmonious environment in my apartment where I could go and relax?

Fuck no!

In East St. Louis, if you relax too much the next thing you know somebody's shoveling dirt in your face.

*   *   *

The meal we had was very simple, a bowl of rice and some steamed vegetables. It tasted all right for what it was and made for a good snack. To tell you the truth though, I'm a meat man myself. Every time that I eat I like to know that some critter that I'm crunching up with my teeth had to die so that I could go on living.

I'm all for a kinder, gentler world but don't you even dream about taking away my red meat. If I get to missing red meat too much, I might put you on the menu.

* * *

After lunch Mai Lin packed an overnight bag, and with her sitting in front with me and pointing the way, we headed on down the road toward the frontier border of Tehan Setar.

CHAPTER 34

The roads didn't get any better with Mai Lin guiding us. If it was possible, they got worse.

We passed people plowing in muddy fields with water buffalo. At least they looked like they were plowing to me. I couldn't figure out anything else they'd be doing out there wading around in that crap all day.

After driving through this farmland for about two or maybe three hours, the road veered into a tree cover and suddenly we were in the jungle.

The farther I drove into that jungle the darker it got. The trees grew thick, and on all sides of us we could hear the calls of strange exotic birds, and the screams of animals that the three of us from the states couldn't even come close to identifying.

One scream came from close to the right side of the car. So close I almost swerved to the left reacting to the sound of it.

It was answered by another one on the other side of the car but further off. Another screech answered that one then another answered that one. The animal screams called back and forth until the entire jungle seemed alive with howls and hoots and screeches.

"What the fuck are those things?" Ron asked.

"Just monkeys," Mai Lin told him.

"I'm glad they're not tigers or some shit like that," Candi said.

"We do have big cats here," Mai Lin told Candi. "But I do not worry about hearing them. By the time you would hear one of our tigers, it would be too late to stop him from eating you."

That was a comforting thought.

* * *

The jungle stretched on and I drove on that lonely, single lane road for a few more hours before night fell over us like a morticians shroud.

You'd think the jungle would get quieter when night came, actually it was the opposite. Bugs and birds that were afraid to make a noise in the daylight raised hell as soon as it got completely dark.

We came to a wide place in the road and Mai Lin told me to pull over and stop. I did and we dug out a few flashlights from our bags and took a look around.

The woods weren't as thick as they looked like from the road, seeing only with the Subaru's headlights. About twenty yards from the road there was a clearing that would be large enough to build a fire and lay our sleeping bags around.

"It will be safe to sleep out here tonight," Mai Lin told us. "Almost no one drives on these roads at night and a fire will keep the animals away."

"I hope so," Candi told us. "I don't want to be no animals dark meat midnight snack."

"What if I bite you in the dark?" Ron asked.

"Well, you are an animal," Candi told him as she and Ron gathered firewood. "But I think I'll make an exception and let you get away with it."

*   *   *

After about fifteen minutes we had a good sized fire burning. We sat around the fire listening to the sounds of the night creatures just beyond the glow of the flames, and every now and then caught the sight of glowing eyes as they passed by our campsite.

Mai Lin asked Ron, "I understand why John has to take revenge for what was done to his woman, but why are you with him?"

"Sherry was family," Ron answered simply. "She was a good woman who was done very wrong. Somebody's got to pay."

Mai Lin looked at Candi.

"Where he goes, I go," Candi said, throwing her arm around Ron. "That's how it is. That's how it's gonna be."

I looked at Mai Lin. "What's your story?" I asked her. "You speak mighty smooth English to be just a Thai country girl."

Mai Lin smiled. "I did grow up in the village where my store is, but my father worked hard to be able to send his children to school in Bangkok. He wished for a better life for us than the one he had.

"He sent my brother and I to live with relatives in the capitol, and when the time came I even attended the university. I fell in love and married a man who, after a time, began lying to me and spending his nights with prostitutes.

"We divorced and I returned to the village where life is simpler. I like being able to look in a person's face and believing what they say is true. In my village, I can live like that."

Mai Lin leaned toward me then and looked deeply into my eyes. She said, "John, I know what you want is revenge, but what you really need to do is to heal."

I considered what she said for a moment and told her, "For somebody who ran away from an education and a chance at a better life, you're acting like you know a whole lot about what other people need. It looks to me like you're somebody who needs to do some healing. Before you can fix somebody else, maybe you should learn how to fix yourself first."

CHAPTER 35

The next morning Ron took over the driving for a while. I was glad he did because my ass was starting to wear out that driver's seat.

Mai Lin sat beside him in the front and told him what turns he needed to make. Every now and then she'd glance back at me over the seat and give me strange, long looks.

I didn't know what the hell was in her head. I didn't know if I'd insulted her when I told her to get her shit together before she tried to tell me what I needed to do. I didn't really give a shit either.

She volunteered to guide us to the border. I hadn't hired her to be me psychiatrist. What she thought didn't matter to me.

Sometime around four PM we came out of the jungle and were back among open fields again. The difference with these fields and the ones we'd passed through before was that there were no farmers here.

Mai Lin explained that we were in territory now that was in dispute. Neither Thailand nor Tehan Setar had solid claims to this land. Because of this most farmers would not settle here. They didn't want to be in the middle of a border war if one broke out.

After about an hour of this kind of land we pulled over and Candi took over the wheel. She wanted to try her hand at driving a car that steered from the right hand side.

She didn't run us off the road or into anything, so it must not have bothered her too much.

When evening was falling we came to a shallow river that Mai Lin said was named The Phao River. That's where we stopped for the night.

*   *   *

Just like we'd done the night before we had a meal of some of the camping food we brought and me and Ron and Candi took turns at watch, each of us doing three hours a piece.

I took the first watch.

Nothing much happened. Bugs buzzed my head. I found a dead tree and broke off some branches and built the fire a little higher.

Ron and Candi shared the same sleeping bag. They'd told Mai Lin she could use one of theirs and they didn't seem to mind cuddling up.

Before I knew it, it was time for me to wake Ron up for his three hour stretch at guard duty. He popped open a Coke we'd packed and set back against a rock and got comfortable.

I dragged my sleeping bag out away from the fire into the shadows. The light and the crackling sounds from the campfire kept me awake the night before. I didn't want to have that happen again.

Out here, among a few clumps of weeds that gave a little bit of cushioning to the hard ground, crickets or whatever the hell these bugs were over here, chirped out to me. They sang a song of the wild lands and the simple life. That song, and the cool night breeze, and the stars like glittering jewels thrown across the sky, were soothing to me.

I drifted, floating, and let my mind sail on the wind. Everything felt peaceful and calm and darkness came down over me.

I felt her against me, the smooth softness of her skin and the soft silk of her hair. The scent of her skin, her hair, her breath filled me. I drew her to me and kissed her on the mouth over and over. The yearning inside of me was overpowering.

She whispered on my ear, "John, I need you."

I kissed her again and said, "Oh god, how I miss you, Sherry."

She stiffened in my arms and I realized that the scent was different; the texture of the skin and hair was different. This was not Sherry in my arms.

This was not a dream.

Mai Lin was here. She was the woman I held.

"I'm sorry," I told her and a tear ran down my cheek.

She touched the tear with her fingertip then kissed the spot where it had been.

"It is OK," Mai Lin said. "I just wish someone would love me the way you loved her."

"Someone will," I told her.

"Perhaps," Mai Lin said. "Maybe it will be you. Maybe when you are done with what you have to do, you will come back to my village?"

I didn't answer her. Mai Lin's offer was tempting but I didn't know if I could ever love anyone ever again.

We held each other in the darkness until the night passed away.

CHAPTER 36

In the morning, when all of us were awake and feeling like moving out, we took a good look at The Phao River. It was wide and shallow. The river was shallow enough so that we could wade across but it was too deep for the car to make it.

"Are there any bridges across this?" I asked Mai Lin.

"None close to here," she answered, "And all the bridges would have armed guards. This is one of the natural land marks that define the border between Thailand and Tehan Setar. When you cross The Phao you will most certainly be within the borders of Tehan Setar."

"Are you in the mood for a good hike?" Ron asked Candi.

"I can walk you in the dirt," Candi told him.

"Do you know roughly where Tehan Setar City is from here?" I asked Mai Lin.

"If you head directly east following the road that is on the other side of The Phao, it is about thirty miles," Mai Lin told us.

We started packing our supplies inside our three duffle bags and Ron asked Mai Lin, "Do you know how to drive?"

"Of course," she answered. "I learned in Bangkok."

He tossed the keys to the Subaru to her.

"Since we're on foot now we won't need this car anymore," Ron told her.

"What will I do with this car?" Mai Lin asked.

"Well," Ron told her. "Start by driving back home, then if you need to go somewhere, drive it there, then keep on driving it anywhere you need to go until the fucking wheels fall off."

"I cannot pay you for it," Mai Lin told him.

Candi told her, "Don't let that bother you. That ain't Ron's car. He doesn't give a shit what happens to it."

*　*　*

We said our good-byes to Mai Lin on the Western shore of The Phao. She wished me good luck and gave me a long, lingering look that said more than spoken words ever could.

As I stepped into the slow current of the cool waters of The Phao River, I knew if I went back to Mai Lin's village I would have the love of a good woman waiting for me. In her village I could find a relatively peaceful life and never want again for someone to love and hold.

I knew I would never go back. Peace and contentment just ain't in the cards for me.

*　*　*

The water only came up to my waist and it felt so good that after we reached the far shore I went back in and dove under to get completely cooled off.

Ron and Candi did the same thing and it wasn't long before we went dripping on down the dirt road that Mai Lin told us would be waiting for us.

On both sides of the road were more of those flooded fields where rice was being grown. There were a lot of smaller roads that lead into this one and after about an hour of walking a guy coming off of his field gave us a ride in his ox pulled cart.

Two hours after that he came to a village where we gave him some cash and he went on his way.

This walking and ox cart riding was too damned slow. We needed a car.

In the village, there was a place to eat and get a beer and three cars were parked outside it. We went in and had Candi ask who owned the cars. One of the guys at the bar draining a beer said that the brown Honda hatchback was his.

He came outside with us and we started his car. It seemed to run good but the inside smelled like beer vomit.

We gave him fifteen hundred dollars and drove with the windows down and the air conditioner running full blast.

Just before dark we arrived at Tehan Setar City.

CHAPTER 37

Where Bangkok had been a huge exotic metropolis, where you actually had to go out and look for the grimy sections of town, in Tehan Setar City you didn't have to look for the ghetto. The entire city looked rundown and decaying. This entire place was a slum.

Except for the smell inside the Honda, I was kind of glad I was driving an old beat-up rust bucket. A new car would stand out here like a sore thumb. This piece of shit on wheels was right at home among all the boarded up businesses and falling down houses.

One other thing, besides the city slowly crumbling, was obvious to us once we entered the streets of this city. The child sex trade was alive and well in Tehan Setar City. Here there were streets after streets of clubs that advertised Boys For Sale, Girls For Sale, Kiddies Under 10 For Your Pleasure. The guys that went in those clubs had to have something wrong with them. If you have any decency at all in you the one thing you don't do is mess around with children.

The laws in this country, if there were any laws at all, must be warped all out of shape.

We needed some directions so I pulled over and parked in a gas station, went in and bought a city map. I was glad the map was bilingual and that they accepted Thai money.

Back in the car we located Udon Way, the street that The St. Wisdom Orphanage was on, and headed over there.

*   *   *

Night descended over this city of lost children as I drove to The St. Wisdom Orphanage. One thing that struck me was that it seemed like the same types of people were on the streets at night that were on the streets during the day. In the American cities that I know, the night people were a different breed than the day people. Except for families getting groceries or going to a movie, the night people were usually predatory types out hunting for something.

The night people were people going to nightclubs or bars, looking for love in all the wrong places, or drug dealers or drug buyers or some other type of criminal looking to cash in under the cover of darkness.

When we arrived at The St. Wisdom Orphanage, the first thing it reminded me of was old pictures I'd seen of The Alamo in San Antonio, Texas. The orphanage was a large square stone structure with high walls all the way around it. It had a huge thick wooden door at the front, with a big steel knocker in its center, and a sliding peep hole.

Over the door there was a plaque that read in two languages The St. Wisdom Orphanage, A Sanctuary For Children From A Harsh World.

I used the knocker and banged hard on the metal strike plate.

After two long minutes went by, the peep hole slid open, and an old lady's watery eyes looked out at us.

The old lady inside spoke something to us in Thai and Candi said something back that ended in Sherry St. Claire.

"Oh, so you are from America," the old lady answered, with a thick cultured British accent. "I should have known immediately, but my eyes aren't what they used to be, and my mind is not quite as sharp either."

The peep hole slid shut. We heard the latch undone and the big wooden door swung inward.

The lady that greeted us was a small white haired woman who wore a black nun's habit. She beamed a smile at us and gave each of us a brief hug as we came in through the door.

"It is so nice to hear from someone who knows Sherry," she told us. "I am Sister Mary Sheridon. I welcome you to our home. Please follow me. We can talk in my office."

The inside of this building was well lit and decorated with religious figures and paintings. It had the look of a Catholic Monastery with one difference. On the walls mixed in with the pictures of Christ and the Saints were pictures that were obviously painted by children.

Looking through the windows as we walked down a corridor to Sister Mary Sheridon's office, we could see that the structure of the entire orphanage was that of a large square building with a spacious central courtyard. Nothing was luxurious about how the place was built or decorated but everything was immaculately clean.

We arrived at the Sister's office. She led us in and motioned us to sit in chairs around her desk.

"Tell me," she said to us as we sat down, "How is Sherry getting along? She was one of our success stories, and Sherry was always one of my personal favorites out of all the girls that have grown up here."

I looked at Ron and Candi and they looked at me. This was going to be hard.

In the past, when I would have deserved to be called a bastard, I would have enjoyed telling this woman that someone she loved was gone forever. But now I understood the pain she was about to feel and I knew I would never enjoy that again.

The look on our faces gave the news before I uttered a word.

"No, please Lord, no," Sister Mary Sheridon said, before I made a sound.

I went and put my arm around her shoulders.

"Sherry is dead," I told her. "We're here to make someone pay for it."

PART II

WELCOME TO
ANOTHER JUNGLE

CHAPTER 38

When Sister Mary Sheridon regained her composure, I filled her in on the how's and why's of what we were doing in her office at that moment.

"Revenge is not something that I would normally support," she told us. "But in this instance, you will do a greater good by removing those who murdered Sherry than by letting the lord make them pay in his own good time.

"The men who harmed Sherry are doing terrible things. They need to be stopped."

"Where can I find William Po?" I asked the Sister.

"I do not meet him directly," she told us. "He has his men bring us the children that he recovers from The Flesh Pit."

"The Flesh Pit, what's that?" Candi asked.

"There is an exclusive resort in the jungle somewhere, where children are the playthings of perverse foreigners. It is said that other, worse atrocities happen there, but I don't know anything for certain.

"Po's men ambush caravans that supply the stolen children, and the caravans that bring the damaged children out to dump them on the streets of Tehan Setar City. The children that come out of that place are usually traumatized so badly they will never function normally in society. Most we take in become nuns or monks.

"I will have one of the sisters guide you to the bus station where William Po's men bring us the children."

Now it hit me.

Sherry was one of the few success stories.

I asked Sister Mary Sheridon, "Did Sherry go through that?"

"Yes," she answered. "When Sherry was seven her father and mother came to Thailand for a vacation. A sight-seeing tour they were with was attacked by bandits. All the adults were robbed and murdered. The children were sold into slavery. Sherry was unfortunate enough to be pretty. Because of that she ended up in The Flesh Pit."

"When she was twelve she escaped somehow and was picked up by Po's men and brought to me. For two years she could not speak and when she finally did it seemed like she could not stop crying. Every little thing would make her cry. But she got past that too.

"She was a strong little girl. If she had not been, she never would have survived.

"Most of the children who come through The St. Wisdom Orphanage we can never trace their origins, their families are too poor, but Sherry was different. She regained the memories of her former life. Through what she told us and her dental records, we traced her back to her parents; Jean Claude St. Claire and Myong Tokuyama St. Claire. They were French citizens.

"Sherry had no living relatives but her father had been a wealthy businessman. I notified the authorities in France of Sherry's survival, and when she turned eighteen she inherited a sizable fortune. She moved to the United States to start a new life but she never completely forgot what she had been through.

"If you wish to avenge Sherry's death then you must destroy The Flesh Pit and the men who run it. They murdered her just as surely as the man who held the knife."

These were harsh words for an old nun to be saying, and her face looked hard as she said them.

"Whatever we've got to do," I told the Sister, "That's what we'll do."

Sister Mary Sheridon smiled. "Perhaps you yourselves are the instruments of God."

"Yeah," Ron said. "He's not a bad guy to have on your side, especially since we're going to be raising hell on Earth."

*   *   *

Sister Mary Sheridon put us up in a room for the night, and as soon as all the kids were asleep, we made use of one of their large communal shower rooms to let hot water wash the grime away.

In the morning after a breakfast of hot oatmeal with the nuns and children in their cafeteria, a frightened-eyed young nun was assigned the task of guiding us to the bus stop where we would meet with a few of William Po's men. The Sister spoke no English but she would make herself understood by just pointing at where to turn.

The sun was shining brightly as we drove across town to the northern edge of the city. Just as we got to the outskirts, on a corner stood a single story building with a parking lot outside it. People roamed around outside and a bus was parked against the curb.

Our nun motioned me to pull into the lot.

I did and parked.

We all got out and the nun walked toward the people outside the building. We followed close behind. One man leading two children, a boy and a girl, came walking toward her.

The Sister motioned toward us and said something to the man. He said something back and then crossed himself and gave a polite bow. The nun took the children by the hand and led them into the bus station.

The man was short and stocky with a rough looking face. He saw us watch as the Sister and the children walked away.

He broke into a broad grin, "You don't have to worry about her. She always calls a taxi from inside." He spoke heavily accented English. "I am Lu Fan. So you want to join our movement? We can use good men," he said, then he looked at Candi, "and women," he added.

"We're just here to shut down The Flesh Pit," I told Lu Fan, "We're here to kill the people who run it and anyone in our way,"

"Good," Lu Fan answered, "That's what we all want to do."

* * *

Lu Fan was driving a pick-up truck. We followed him in our car about forty miles to a camp in the middle of the jungle.

CHAPTER 39

Tropical birds screeched strange cries down at us from the treetops as we pulled up and stopped just within the boundaries of a small tent city, and when I say small, I mean really small.

There were maybe ten tents spread among the trees and bushes, a few fires that people were cooking from, and a few guys were cleaning guns or sharpening knives and that was it.

We got out of the Honda Hatchback and I went to Lu Fan. I was wearing a light jacket even though it was hot as hell. I had my right hand in the jacket pocket gripping my .38.

"I want to speak to William Po," I said.

"In time you will know him," Lu Fan answered. "For now, you must wait."

"I don't believe in waiting," I told Lu Fan. "It cannot be avoided."

Ron said, "Then whoever's in charge here, we need to talk to him."

At that moment, the flap to the tent closest to us-- a big eight man job-- slid open and a wiry looking man in his forties, with steely eyes and a harsh expression, came out.

"This is the man in charge," Lu fan said, and took us to him.

Some words in Thai passed between them. The man turned to us. "The Flesh Pit is something we all wish to destroy. What qualifies you to do what we have not been able?"

"I was a Search and Destroy Specialist with the US Military Forces in Viet Nam," I said. "Our job was finding specific Viet Cong military leaders; infiltrate their camps and kill them. A few missions I was on involved destroying POW camps. Do you have anyone better qualified?"

"No, I do not," he answered. "But a more important question is why should we trust you?"

"The Sisters sent them," Lu Fan cut in.

"And," I said, to the leader of these homeless freedom fighters, as I brought the .38 out of my jacket pocket, "If we weren't on your side, you'd be dead already."

The man smiled then.

"I cannot argue with that logic," he said.

*   *   *

We followed the leader into the tent. He told us, "Here, I am simply called Jong. My name is Wanna Kit Wachirabangjong."

"Then Jong it is," I told him and introduced myself, then Ron and Candi.

Jong got right to the point then. "With so many evil men in your homeland why do you come this far to fight the evil here?"

I explained about hunting Sherry's killer and ended with, "A man named Tian Kham is the one who murdered her. Have you heard of him?"

"I have heard the name. He is one of the overlord's assassins."

"Who is this overlord?" Ron asked.

"We do not know exactly who he is," Jong told us. "The Overlord is a name we use for the man who owns and runs The Flesh Pit, and sends out his men to buy children wherever they can find them."

Candi said, "Since everyone seems to be throwing out questions I need to get mine in, even if it might seem a little stupid to everybody else here." She looked at Jong.

"Go ahead."

"Well, this jungle fighting against child sex slavers doesn't seem to be something you'd take up as a weekend hobby. So how did you end up doing this anyway?"

Jong's face clouded and he looked at the dirt in front of his feet.

"I am trying to atone for the greatest shame of my life by giving my life to a good cause. I was a farmer, a poor man when a man came to our village offering to pay for our children to work in his factory. He said he would board them and feed them well and return them at the end of three months.

"Many in my village took his offer. I sold him our daughter. He gave us an address, a phone number, and the money. I gave my daughter a kiss on the forehead and told her to be a good girl and do what she was instructed to do. I'll never forget the trusting smile she gave me. My daughter wanted to make me proud of her. The man drove away with our children in the back of his truck.

"When I tried to call to find out how my daughter was getting along, the phone number was no good. I then found out the factory and address he left with us did not exist.

"The police will do nothing. Our government will do nothing. Here, as well as everywhere, money makes you powerful. We are poor people. Our voices will not be heard.

"In despair my wife took her own life. I pray the lord forgives her. She could not stand the pain of what I had done. I sold our daughter.

"This is the only life that is left for me now. My daughter is gone forever. I do not know if she is alive or dead. I only know that men like the Overlord have taken her away from me. The Overlord and men like him must pay for what they do."

"That's what we're here for," I told Jong, "To make sure that he does."

CHAPTER 40

Jong told us the approximate location of The Flesh Pit. It didn't matter that he wasn't very specific. The Flesh Pit was in the middle of the jungle and there was only one road in and out so we'd have to be guided there anyway.

Since there was only one road, we couldn't use it.

We had to go on foot. That was the only way to get to The Flesh Pit without everyone knowing that we were coming.

Jong drew us a rough diagram of what the place looked like in the dirt. It was a relatively simple set up. There were five main buildings and a large paved open area that served as a helicopter landing pad.

The entire complex was separated from the rest of the world by a fifteen foot tall chain link fence topped by razor wire.

It was not an easy place to get into or out of.

The children and supplies were always brought in by the road. The guests always paid top dollar for the privilege of going there and raping the kids. Guests were brought in and taken out by helicopter.

Jong estimated that thirty guards were on the complex all the time. They had their own quarters. It was next to the place where the children were locked up.

Other than that there was the hotel where the guests and the staff that ran The Flesh Pit stayed, a two story night club named appropriately, The Flesh Pit, and a health spa.

I'd need to see the place first hand before I could come up with a plan for how to get in and destroy it.

I asked Jong what kind of weapons his men had.

He said, "most have rifles. A few have pistols. All of them have knives."

"Do you have any explosives?" I asked.

"No, nothing like that," he answered.

This was looking pretty fucking bleak.

"Look," I told Jong, "My woman sent a lot of money over here to William Po. What the fuck have you been doing with it?" I felt like busting this guy upside the head, but that wouldn't help anything so I didn't do it. I knew Jong wasn't at fault for anything, but this damn jungle heat made you feel like beating the crap out of somebody, whether you had a good reason or not.

"Any money that comes in goes to a central bank account. I can get small amounts out," Jong said. "I use as little as possible. Most times I only get enough for food.

"The Flesh Pit is not the only place of its kind. There are many, and we are not the only group of William Po's men. There are many groups throughout the countries in this region. The money that comes in does not go far."

I knew he was telling the truth so I didn't press him any further about it.

*   *   *

The next morning we took an inventory of the tools that everyone had to see what could be useful. The only thing that looked like something we could use was a heavy duty pair of wire cutters. The wire cutters were big enough to cut through a chain link fence. We'd take those with us.

CHAPTER 41

Around noon we asked for volunteers from Chong's men to go and hit The Flesh Pit.

Six stepped forward. One extra man was assigned to go with us to stay behind and guard the three cars we'd leave at the point where we'd have to go on foot. He was supposed to stay with the cars for a week then give us up for dead.

* * *

After driving for two hours of lonely dirt roads we came to the edge of a jungle, where the road came to a sudden end. We stopped and unpacked our gear.

The hot sun beat down on us, and in the distance four elephants picked fruit and leaves from trees to eat. It was a primordial scene that had been replayed here endlessly for at least the last thousand years. It was a reminder that here we were isolated.

* * *

We marched all day through the steaming jungle, keeping our eyes wide open for anything that was going on around us. Out here armed bandits were just one thing we had to worry about. Out here there were all kinds of animals and snakes that could kill you and eat you.

Lu Fan told us that normally tigers avoid people as much as they can. That was fine with me. I wanted to avoid them, too.

When it got dark we camped and made a fire and with a guard posted we slept as well as we could. It wasn't too damned good either.

* * *

By noon the next day we were close enough to The Flesh Pit to drop our gear, and me and Lu Fan went forward to scout it out alone. I was carrying my AKS-74U and my .38. Lu Fan had his rifle. We were hoping we didn't have to use these yet.

Two men alone can remain unseen. With ten men, during the daytime, somebody would probably be spotted. We circled around keeping the tree line between us and the high chain link fence. The place was as Jong had described it; five buildings and a helicopter landing pad. The high fence was topped with razor wire and the only posted guard was at the front gate.

The only other guards we saw were two guys that were walking the edge of the fence. Jong had told us to expect four.

One other thing that was different was that the helicopter was gone.

When I whispered to Lu Fan that there was less security than we expected he answered, "There must be no guests here now. Maybe that's why they have fewer guards out."

We'd made a complete circle of the compound and were near the front gate when a Jeep drove up the dirt road and slid to a stop.

The man that got out and yelled for the guard to open the gate was the same man who I'd seen in the video tape cut Sherry's throat. It was Tian Kham.

It was all I could do to stop myself from coming out from behind those trees and riddling his body with bullets. But that would be too fast for him. I wanted to get that son-of-a-bitch in a position where I could make his death slow and painful, something he could relive endlessly in hell.

CHAPTER 42

We went back to the camp that we'd made about a quarter mile from The Flesh Pit and told everyone what we'd found. This little military operation was looking easier than we'd expected. We'd just snip the fence with the cutters, get in, cut some throats and take over. It looked like a piece of cake.

I should have known better.

With lookouts posted, we tried to catch some shut eye as we waited for night to fall. With knowing what was ahead of us, sleep didn't come easy.

*   *   *

Nighttime fell like a brick out of the sky. Maybe it seemed to come so fast because the jungle was always in shadow. I don't know. It just seemed like one minute it was light, the next minute it was pitch black.

We had Lu Fan guide us to The Flesh Pit. Out in the jungle in the darkness, the three of us from America would have gotten lost in a heartbeat.

When we were on the other side of the tree line from the chain link fence, Lu Fan told us that he wanted to make one more circle around the compound to be certain of where the guards were.

"It will only take me a few minutes," he told us. "A saying that you Americans use fit what we are doing: it is better to be safe than sorry."

"Then get to it," I told him. "If you're not back in fifteen minutes, I'm cutting that fence and going in."

With our backs to an Asian Jungle, watching for any movement at all in the mostly darkened facility named The Flesh Pit, the ten minutes that Lu Fan was gone seemed like hours.

He came back sliding through the grass as silent as a snake. "One guard is sleeping," he told us. "The other one I saw enter the health spa with a very attractive teenage girl. I believe he will be preoccupied for some time. We should move now. The Flesh Pit is essentially unguarded."

I told two of the rebels to stay outside the fence and watch our backs. I crawled forward clutching the wire cutters in one hand with my AKS-74U slung over my back.

At the fence I took a good look around. I didn't see anything moving at all. The lack of movement and the silence had my nerves jangling, and that was the way I wanted them to be.

I quickly cut the strands of fencing along the bottom near the ground three feet long, and then paused to freeze and scan the area around me again.

No movement, nothing.

I cut the fencing right up the middle to make a flap three feet high and signaled to Ron and Candi. I slid through the flap and waited on the other side.

Just like we'd planned, Ron ran up and grabbed the fencing and bent it up. Candi came running in a crouch. She got to the fence, flattened herself to the ground, and squeezed through the gap.

Ron stayed holding the fence up and four more of the William Po men slid through the hole I'd made and joined us on the other side.

The only other man we had planned to have inside was Lu Fan, but I could see now he wasn't coming. He was trying to get our two lookouts to follow us on through the hole in the fence.

That wasn't in the plan that we'd come up with together today.

"Get your ass over here," Ron whispered as loudly as he could at Lu Fan, and waved him forward.

"What the hell is up with him?" Candi whispered to me.

Her question was answered immediately.

Floodlights came on from the rooftops pinning us to the ground.

"Drop your weapons," a bull horn shouted at us.

I jumped to my feet and fired off a stream of bullets into one of the lights. It winked out.

The sound of Ffffffft shot past my head and several more of those followed. I didn't know what the hell was making that noise and I didn't want to find out.

We were like deer in the headlights waiting for the crash.

156

Something stung me in the back.

I spun toward it and fired, hitting nothing.

The rebels were firing blindly and I saw two of them go down simultaneously.

Over at the fence, Ron was on his knees pulling something out of his left shoulder and screaming out a string of curses at his unseen assailants.

That son-of-a-bitch Lu Fan had to have set us up because now he was firing at our two lookouts.

I went to run and my legs were numb.

Two more stings hit me, one in the stomach and one in the chest.

My legs wouldn't move. I fell hard on my face and rolled over. I went to bring my rifle up to shoot and my arms wouldn't move.

The world was swimming around me. I was moving in super slow motion or not at all.

I heard Candi scream, "Leave him alone!" I doubt she was talking about me.

The Fffffftt's had stopped and none of our guys were firing either.

From my back I saw three men walk into the glare of the spot lights. One was Lu Fan. Another was Tian Kham. The other one was a silver haired Caucasian man dressed in a three piece suit.

The white man turned to Lu Fan. "I told you to get them all within the fence," he barked at him.

"I tried," Lu Fan answered. "They would not listen to me. We will track them down in the jungle."

"That's not good enough," The man told Lu Fan. "I pay for total obedience. I get total obedience!"

"I will try harder next time," Lu Fan said.

"There is no next time," The white man said, and looked at Tian Kham and nodded.

Tian Kham stepped back, drew a pistol from inside his jacket, put the barrel to the side of Lu Fan's head and pulled the trigger.

Lu Fan's head exploded.

Even with the bright white of a spotlight shining into my eyes, the night came down and claimed me.

CHAPTER 43

There's a burning in my nostrils like something fowl smelling being shoved up my nose. My eyes flashed open and Tian Kham is holding smelling salts to my face. I came awake suddenly and tried to stand. My wrists were tied to the arms of a movie theater style seat. I jerked at the ropes holding me but they didn't give one bit.

Tian Kham smiled. "Good, you are awake now," he said. "You can enjoy the show."

Shit! I thought. *Why didn't I just kill this asshole when I saw him at the gate and get it over with?*

"I know why you are here," Tian Kham said. "You come for revenge. Perhaps being without the woman makes your life not worth living. If that is the case, then I will do you the favor of ending your miserable life."

I jerked at the ropes that held me some more, trying to rip the arms off the seat I was in, and failed. "Then get to it," I told him. "There ain't shit you can do that I ain't seen before."

"Perhaps," he said. "But we are here for entertainment and your deaths will entertain us."

He strode off and I looked around me.

This place was a type of small stadium. Rows upon rows of seats were placed in a circular pattern bolted to the cement steps of a bowl-like structure. Down at the bottom was a large eight sided fenced in cage. Right now they had two little girls inside the cage slinging punches at each other.

At the top of the highest row of seating two television style cameras on opposite sides of the cage, filmed everything that happened.

Ron and Candi were sitting beside me, and beside them were the four William Po men who came through the fence with us. I was probably the last one they woke up with the smelling salts.

We were in the row of seats closest to the cage, and looking through the fenced walls I could see that there were perhaps seventy spectators here.

There was not one full grown woman among the crowd in the seats. All the spectators looked like they were middle aged men. Most of them had young boys and girls sitting with them that they openly fondled.

Straight across from us, sitting among this crowd of middle aged perverts, on what could only be described as a throne, was the silver haired man who I'd seen beside Tian Kham when he'd executed Lu Fan.

He had a bull horn in his hand. He raised it to his lips. He looked over at us. "Our uninvited guests have awakened from their beauty rest," he announced into the megaphone. "Get the girls out of the cage and let's show them how welcomed they are."

A man went into the cage and stopped the girls from battling. He ushered them out.

Two men appeared with pistols at the far end of the line from where I was. One put his pistol to the head of the William Po man who was last in line.

The other untied the rebel's arms from the chair. They took him to the end of the row of seats and shoved him to the gate of the cage. The one in front unlocked the cage door and he was shoved inside.

The man with the megaphone spoke again, "These men would come and take away from you the hard earned right to pay for any pleasure you see fit to purchase. They think they have the God-given right to do this. I think not.

"The ancients had a way of letting The Almighty choose who was right in matters of morals. They called it Trial by Combat."

"The winner lives. The loser dies. The Almighty rules all destinies so he chooses who is right and who is wrong.

"With that I give you our representative in this contest of conflicting morals.

"Tarkus!"

The crowd clapped and cheered, and from a door high above the rows of seats emerged a giant of a man. He stood easily over six feet seven and weighed somewhere in the neighborhood of two hundred and sixty pounds.

This representative of warped divine justice looked like an escapee from the World Wrestling Federation. He had muscles on top of muscles and long black hair that hung down over a permanently scowling face.

He bounded down the steps and threw open the door to the cage and jumped inside.

The William Po man inside was a skinny little dude. He was outweighed by at least a hundred and twenty pounds.

"Shit!" I told Ron and Candi. "This ain't gonna be no fucking contest."

"There'll be one when they get to me," Ron barked out. Then he yelled to the silver haired guy who Tian Kham was now sitting beside, "Put him in with me. Let the mother-fucker fuck with somebody his own size!"

They ignored Ron.

In the cage, Tarkus moved toward the William Po man who backed off and ran around the edge of the cage along the fence. Tarkus chased him for a few steps then just stopped and looked at the man on the throne and waved his hand in the air like he was saying, "This guy ain't shit."

The William Po man took that opportunity to run at the big man from behind and kicked him a good one in the leg. When Tarkus turned the William Po man unloaded a whole series of karate like blows into the stomach and chest of his opponent.

Tarkus didn't even move.

He grabbed the William Po man by the hair of the head with his left hand and lifted him straight up in the air. Tarkus drew back his huge right fist and slammed it into the little guy's face. The sound of breaking bones and snapping teeth was heard.

The William Po man's legs kicked a few times then he went limp. Blood poured from his nose and mouth, and several teeth fell and bounced on the concrete flooring.

Tarkus hoisted the unconscious William Po man up over his head with both arms, and then slammed him down to the concrete as hard as he could. The little freedom fighter landed with a crunch and did not move again.

"Bring me more!" Tarkus bellowed to the man on the throne as the dead man was dragged out.

The other three William Po men were forced at gunpoint down into the cage.

As soon as the cage door closed the three yelled some kind of battle cry and simultaneously charged the goliath in front of them. The problem was he charged them too.

The two William Po men on both sides of Tarkus were clothes-lined flying from their feet. The other one, Tarkus just plain ran over and stomped beneath his boots.

The one that went underfoot was totally out. The other two were seeing stars and were slowly trying to get their wits about them and regain their feet.

Tarkus grabbed the unconscious guy by both ankles and slung him up in the air like a kid with a Raggedy Andy Doll that was having a temper tantrum. He slung the rebel freedom fighter up over his head and then reversed direction like a man splitting fire wood with an ax, and bashed in the head of a William Po man who was still on his knees with the head of the guy he was using for a club.

The cracking together of their skulls sounded like a rock being used to crack open a coconut shell. The man on the cement started twitching all over like his brain wasn't sending out the right signals to his body.

Tarkus bashed him again to make him lay still, and then threw the bloody bag of rags that had once been a man at the remaining William Po man, who had just made it to a standing position.

The last rebel fighter was knocked sprawling into the fence. When he tried to get back up, Tarkus body checked him into the fence. Then he slammed a hard elbow into his face.

Bones snapped and blood flew.

The crowd cheered. As a matter of fact they'd been cheering nonstop since this whole bloody spectacle began.

Tarkus grabbed the William Po man up and hoisted him over his head, then drove him down head first into the concrete. The rebel started kicking and jerking all over the place so Tarkus leaped onto his chest. Then he jumped up and down caving in his chest cavity until the little guy was about as thick as a well-worn shag carpet.

"You ain't shit!" Ron yelled at the big guy.

Candi leaned over and whispered to him, "Honey, don't piss this guy off, OK?"

"Fuck! They're going to kill us anyway," Ron said. "Before I go, I want to get me a piece of the biggest and ugliest mother-fucker that they've got, and I think that's him."

Ron yelled again, "Come on you bastard! Fight someone your own size. I know why all you fucking idiots have to screw with children. You don't have what it takes to satisfy an adult. You fucking disgust me, you sick sons-of-bitches!"

Hell, Ron was taking all my best lines. That's fine. Today, he could have them.

Tarkus looked to where we were and pointed at Ron. He spoke to the silver haired man on the throne. "I want him," he shouted.

The bull horn was used again. The man on the throne spoke, "I was going to save these three for tonight's show, but what do my guests want?"

As one, the crowd shouted that they wanted more blood.

When the soldiers were coming to untie Ron, he leaned over and told Candi, "I love you babe. I always will."

"I love you," Candi told him.

Then they walked Ron Martin at gunpoint into the cage.

CHAPTER 44

The instant that Ron entered the cage the difference in build between him and Tarkus was obvious.

Even at six foot five Ron was stocky and built heavy. He was an ex-football player and was built perfect for that sport.

Tarkus was at least two inches taller than Ron and he was ripped. Veins popped out on Tarkus' arms every time that he moved.

Where Ron looked to be in pretty good shape for a guy of his size, Tarkus looked like he lived in the weight room and did isometrics about as often as he breathed. Tarkus was built and moved like a highly conditioned prizefighter. Ron, well he was a big strong son-of-a-bitch and that was about it.

Ron rushed Tarkus and was met by a side thrust kick to the chest that knocked him backward.

Tarkus rushed Ron and was met with an NFL style body block that knocked him into the fence.

Tarkus circled to the left side and snapped a left jab at Ron's face. Ron slipped underneath it and was met by a rising knee that brought him out of his crouch.

Tarkus backed off again and motioned Ron forward.

It was obvious to me that Tarkus' tactics were going to be to circle and stab at Ron from a distance. He had the height and reach and quickness to make it work, too. I was hoping that Ron knew what Tarkus was planning for him. The thing was, even if he did, it might not make a difference anyway.

I took a look at Candi and her face was like stone. She wasn't going to let any of these idiots know how seeing Ron get his ass kicked was affecting her.

And Ron was starting to take an ass whipping. Ron learned from eating that knee that he couldn't just rush in with his head down. He had to be more selective with his aggression.

Tarkus was teaching Ron why he couldn't just stand back and wait also. Tarkus moved toward him, snapping out leg kicks and following with long straight punches.

One of the punches busted open a cut over Ron's left eye that spurted blood. A kick busted his lips and made his nose bleed.

After Ron tried rushing Tarkus a few more times and only meeting knuckles and shoe leather from his back-peddling opponent, he was lost for what else he should do.

That was when Tarkus started taunting him. He started yelling, "American Pig! American Coward!" And pointing at Ron as he was doing it.

Blood was pouring down Ron's face from at least a half dozen cuts. Ron smiled through the cuts. He yelled beck, "If I'm a fucking coward then why you keep running? Stand still and fight me, you fucking punk!"

Tarkus kept up his circling and after Ron ate a good left-right, Ron started keeping his hands up in front of his face. Ron also started pawing at his nose with his left hand as he followed Tarkus around the cage.

I was just figuring he had a broken nose that he was trying to set at the same time as he was fighting. I found out I was wrong.

Ron had taken to putting his hands up high whenever Tarkus threw the jab out, but the last time he surprised me, and sure as hell surprised Tarkus, by just eating the jab and flinging his left hand out blindly in the direction of Tarkus face.

A handful of blood and snot shot out from Ron's hand and splattered into Tarkus' eyes.

Tarkus threw his hands up to his eyes and Ron barreled into him, grabbing him in a bear hug. Then Ron lifted Tarkus from the floor and slammed him down to the cement.

Tarkus' head made a loud pop as it struck the cement and he went stiff. Ron rolled Tarkus over with a wrestling move, then mounted his back, and, grabbing him by the hair of the head, he pounded his face into the floor.

"Let's see how you fucking like this," Ron yelled at him, as he broke Tarkus' nose and teeth on the cement.

The cheering suddenly stopped. The place was silent except for Ron's shouts and the sound of Tarkus head bouncing off the floor.

When Tarkus was totally unconscious, Ron reached down and picked up Tarkus' head in his hands, and then looked up to the man on the throne. "It's a little different when your boy has to take a bit, isn't it?"

Then he wrenched to the side, trying to make Tarkus do an impersonation of Linda Blaire in The Exorcist. It didn't work. Tarkus' neck broke before his head swiveled half the way around.

Ron stood up off of Tarkus and looked back and forth between the two cameramen recording his every movement. He yelled at them, "You can tape this, too," he gave them both the finger. "Fuck you!" Ron shouted.

The man on the throne did not look happy. He locked eyes with Ron. He picked up the megaphone.

"Kill him," he said.

The soldiers outside the fence weren't stupid enough to open the gate. They pointed their rifles at Ron and he shouted curses at them and dared them to come inside.

They opened fire and Ron went down. He tried to get up and they kept firing until he went down again and stopped moving.

Every time a bullet struck Ron, Candi sucked in a breath but she never looked away.

CHAPTER 45

With Ron and Tarkus still laying in the middle of the cage, the spectators filed out of the auditorium. The guy on the throne and Tian Kham went with them. Before they left, Tian Kham gave instructions to some of the guards and six of them came over to where we were still tied to our seats.

As two guards untied our ropes, four of them held rifles on us. I leaned over to Candi and whispered, "Don't do anything. Our chance will come."

One of the guards stepped forward and backhanded me before my arms were loose. He yelled in my face, "Shut up, American Pig!"

I was glad my arms weren't loose yet. If they were I'd have busted that fucker upside the head and got both me and Candi killed. As it was, I just spit out a little blood from a busted lip, grinned at the guard, and let the moment pass.

After we were standing, the guards tied our hands behind us then lead us outside.

On the way, out we went down two flights of stairs then passed rooms with exercise equipment and saunas, and passed by a window that showed a large indoor swimming pool. It was easy to figure out that this was the health spa.

It was day time as we passed outside through the front entrance, and that made me wonder just how long I'd been knocked out from whatever had been in those darts they'd shot us with. Considering it was in the middle of the night when we tried our wreck of a raid, we must have been out for at least twelve hours.

The guards lead us past the guest hotel and past a large night club with a big unlit neon sign that read The Flesh Pit. Then they lead us past the oversized helicopter landing pad that now had a helicopter in the middle of it that looked like a repainted military troop transporter. That must be how they brought in those howling maniacs that cheered on Tarkus until he bit the dust.

The guards took us in the side door of an oblong rectangular building. We were herded down a hallway that had the look of an old time western prison.

On both sides of the hall were rows of cells that were separated by steel bars that were mortared into the floor and ceiling. Children were locked inside the cells. The oldest kid I saw was probably somewhere around twelve or thirteen. The youngest kid I saw in those cells, as unbelievable as it sounds, seemed to be barely old enough to be out of diapers.

All the children had the vacant look of utter hopelessness on their faces. Kids should be running and laughing and having fun, but these kids looked like all the life had been beaten or raped out of them.

The guards put me in one cell then put Candi in the one next to mine. We were separated by a wall of vertical steel bars.

They locked us in and left.

Each cell had a sleeping cot against the wall. Candi went and sat on the cot and stared forward, not saying anything.

I tested the bars of the cell and the swinging door, and then checked out the lock. This might be an old fashioned cell but the steel was heavy. I wasn't The Incredible Hulk so I wasn't going to be knocking these damned bars down and escaping that way.

Candi's quietness was worrying me. I knew she cared about Ron but she didn't seem to be reacting to his death at all. I went to the bars that separated our cells and leaned on them with my hands. I spoke to her.

"I'm sorry about Ron," I told Candi. "I never should have let him get involved in this."

Candi was silent for a moment. Then she looked up at me from where she sat on her cot with burning eyes.

"Ron was a man," Candi said. "He lived the way he wanted to live. He did what he wanted to do. That's why he was with me. He didn't care what people thought about us. He was hunting Sherry's killer because he wanted to. You couldn't have stopped him."

"He was a good man," I told her.

"Yeah," Candi answered. "I know I've lost the best man I'll ever meet."

Candi was quiet, lost inside her own self for a few seconds then she said, "What Ron would want is for us to go on and complete what we started so I can't talk about him anymore. We've got to be strong and make it through this. I can't let myself even shed one tear, because if I start crying, I know I won't be able to stop."

CHAPTER 46

I figured it to be late afternoon or early evening when they took us to our cells because the day seemed to pass extremely fast. We were only just settling back on our cots when a guy came by and slid a bowl of something that looked like vegetable soup through a slot in the bars at floor level.

The bowl that the soup was in was one of those semi-paper things that you use at picnics. The spoon was a plastic spoon. We wouldn't be tunneling out of here anytime soon with this stuff.

I ate the food, which was very bland but it was food, and lay down on the cot to get some rest. It was a little bit after that, that I heard footsteps in the hallway and the sound of two Oriental men laughing and talking back and forth.

It was two of the hired guns. They stopped outside of Candi's cell. Both of these guys were wearing camouflage fatigues and had pistols in holsters on their belts.

One was around five foot nine and a hundred and seventy pounds. The other was a little smaller than he was.

The larger man leered at Candi through the bars and grinned. He put his hand on his pistol.

"Take your clothes off," he barked at her.

Candi got up off the cot she had been laying on and stood up. She locked eyes with the guard.

"I don't think so," she told him in an even voice.

The guard went a little red in the face then he laughed.

"American bitch!" He spit at Candi. "Here, you will do as you are told!"

They unlocked the door to Candi's cell and stepped inside. The larger guard drew his pistol and, stepping forward, transferred it to his left hand.

I went to the bars that separated our cells.

"Leave her alone!" I yelled.

The one advancing toward Candi glanced at me. "This entire building is sound proofed. Shout if you wish. It will make no difference."

The other guard moved into the cell with his back to me.

Candi spoke to the guard again but this time her voice was smooth like flowing honey. "All right, I'll do whatever you want. If I'm going to be here I might as well have some fun too. Come on big boy," she said. "Let me see what you've got."

"Well, well, we've got a lively one this time," the guard who was coming at Candi said to his buddy. "Maybe we found one who likes it rough."

"Oh yeah, now you're speaking my language," Candi told the two of them. "I like it rough. I can make it so rough you'll cum like you've never cum before."

"Get you clothes off," the guard told her again.

"Take them off for me," Candi told him and stepped forward.

He put his right hand up to stop her and she slowly reached both her hands up and took his hand in hers. Then she put his hand on her chest and kneaded her own breast using his hand.

"Oh yeah," Candi breathed. "That's good."

The guard still had his pistol in his left hand but his right hand started working overtime squeezing Candi's breast.

He was breathing heavy and she nuzzled into his neck and kept saying, "Oh yeah, oh yeah."

The other guard's eyes were glued to Candi and his buddy. I was completely forgotten.

Candi started moaning and groaning as the guy ran his hand up and down her body. He ran his hand down around her back then pulled her to him while clutching her ass. Then he slid his hand around the front of her and reached between her legs.

I knew what was coming next.

He shouted, "You got a dick!" and tried to pull away and Candi had his left hand clutched in her right hand.

This was an uneven struggle. Candi was far stronger than the guy she was wrestling with. Keeping the guard between her and his buddy, she wrenched the gun from his left hand and kicked him off of her backward into the other guard.

171

The other guard stumbled backward into the bars separating our cells. I grabbed him by the hair of the head, threw my left arm around his throat, then wrenched his head hard to the side.

Vertebra snapped and he sank to the floor like the bones from his legs had vanished.

The guy who had been feeling Candi up was now on the floor on his hands and knees. Candi had his gun in her hands and she was pointing it at his head.

"Please," he begged her. "Please, please don't kill me. Please show me mercy."

"Not fucking likely," Candi told him, and pulled the trigger, splashing his brains across the cement floor.

CHAPTER 47

Candi got the keys and unlocked my cell. We each took one of the pistols from each of the guards. We stepped out into the hallway between the two rows of cells.

"What now?" Candi asked.

I looked down the long rows of bars on both sides of the hall. A few of the children had taken an interest in what we were doing and were standing up next to the bars watching us.

They all had the same kind of dead eyes, like all the fight had been beaten out of them. They wanted to do something to get out of here but they were just too scared to even ask us to unlock their cages.

A voice came to me from inside my head. It was Sherry's voice. It said, "Save the children!"

How the hell am I supposed to do that? I shot the thought back at her.

She didn't answer my question.

I looked at Candi. "Let's let these kids out," I told her. "We'll figure out our next step after that."

We went down the long hallway unlocking the cells and swinging the doors open. Most of the kids just looked at us and didn't move. They were too shell shocked to even consider the possibility of escaping this hellish life that they were trapped in.

When we had all the doors unlocked a few of the older kids had come out into the hallway and were now looking to us to tell them what to do.

There were eight kids that were standing around us waiting for us to do something.

I turned to Candi, "Do you remember that helicopter outside?"

"Yeah," she answered.

"That's the only way we're getting these kids out of here. Do you think you can fly it?" I asked.

She snorted a laugh. "I ain't never even been in anything like that."

"Shit!" I said.

The kids all looked at me. They wanted ... no, needed somebody to help them.

"All right, fuck-it," I told Candi. "I've ridden in a few of those things in my time. I've even ridden in the co-pilots seat bullshitting with the pilot. If we can make it to that chopper, I'll see if I can get it off the ground.

"I get it in the air and follow the first road I see to the first town. We land there and drop these kids off, and then we come back for some serious payback."

Candi said, "So that's the only plan we got, right? That seems pretty much off the wall."

"It is," I told her. "If you got a better one let me know, because I know we don't have a chance in hell of making this one work."

*　　*　　*

I had one of the kids run and latch the door at the north end of the building. I had another kid go and start dragging the other children out of their cells. I knew it was a suicide mission to try and take all the kids in these cells with us in one mad dash to that helicopter but we had to at least try. Besides, how would you ever decide which ones you would leave behind?

Me and Candi, trailed by an ever growing crowd of children, went to the door on the south end of the building. I opened the door and looked out.

Directly south, about thirty yards away, was the hotel where the guests and the staff stay. To the west were two bushes and a small tree that formed a border between where the guards patrolled the fence line and the guests walked inside the complex. To the east were a couple more decorative bushes, trees, and a walkway, and about fifty yards past that was the helicopter landing pad where the chopper sat.

The thought hit me that since they used that chopper exclusively to haul in their high paying guests for security they probably kept some weapons stored in the helicopter at all times.

If we were to get in a gunfight on the way out, which was highly likely, the two of us needed something better than just these two pistols we were packing.

"I'm going to have to go scout out the best way to get these kids to the chopper," I told Candi. "I need you to stay here and don't let anybody come in through this door."

"You don't have to worry about that," Candi told me. "I am not going back in that cage again. Anyone tries to come through this door and he ain't someone I know, he's dead."

* * *

I slipped out the door and flattened myself against the building.

Evening was falling. It was that in between time, between when it was bright daylight and full night darkness. The bright greens of the day were now starting to look like dull dark grays. All the colors were losing their vibrancy. All the colors were slowly darkening and blending together.

I was hoping the changing of colors from day to night would help me blend in with the surroundings.

Stepping out to the halfway point between the slave quarters where we'd been locked up and the guest hotel, I stopped beside a bush and took a good look. Nobody was moving around that I could see. As I scanned the distance between the slave quarters and the helicopter, looking for the most direct route, that chopper seemed like it was at least fifty miles away.

Out of the corner of my eye I saw movement. Without thinking I dropped to the ground beside the bush.

The two guards walked over the fence. From where I was crouched down I could see everything they did. One spit through the fence. The other one took a deep drag on his cigarette and threw it away. He pulled his pack out of his pocket and made a disgusted sound when he saw that it was empty, then wadded up the empty pack and tossed it over the fence.

I could see all the way across the complex past the edge of the helicopter to the building to where the guards lived. It came to me in a flash. *He's going to come right through here to cut across to go get some cigarettes from his room.*

I glanced at the door into the guest hotel. It was open just a small crack, but it was open.

The guards were still talking and even though it was in a language I didn't understand, I knew as sure as I know the moon was going to shine somewhere on that night that as soon as they stopped talking, one of those guards was going to come right through the bushes where I was crouched down.

On hands and knees I scurried over to the side door into the guest hotel and pushed it open.

I stepped inside and stood up.

CHAPTER 48

There was no one in the hallway and, except for a maid's cart piled high with towels, linen, and cleaning supplies sitting a few doors from this end of the corridor, the hallway was deserted.

I heard a door about midway down creak as it was pulled open. I ran to the maid's cart and crouched down behind it.

The cart that I crouched down beside had shelves that ran all the way through. Most of the shelves were filled with bleaches and detergents and sprays to make everything look spotlessly clean. One of the shelves had an empty space all the way through and with my face bathed on deep shadows I could see who stepped out of the door.

He was a small man. He was Oriental and he had on a Hawaiian shirt. *That bastard must love those Hawaiian shirts. He wears them enough.*

It was Tian Kham, the man who cut Sherry's throat.

He walked directly toward the cart that I hid behind. One door before he got to where I was, he unlocked the door and entered that room.

He left the door open behind him.

* * *

I went to the open doorway. I stood beside it and listened. No voices came from inside. *He must be alone.*

There was no way I was letting this opportunity pass me by. The main reason I came over here was to kill this one man. He wasn't going to leave that room alive.

I slipped inside the door and closed it behind me.

It was a typical hotel room with a large bed, a TV, and a dresser with a mirror.

Tian Kham was standing at the dresser. A drawer was open. The drawer was filled with Hawaiian shirts. He was fingering through the shirts looking for a change.

With the click of the latch as the door shut, Tian Kham spun around and faced me. He saw the gun in me right hand. He smiled.

"I should have expected that you would come for me," he said. "A motivated man is difficult to stop. This was predictable and yet I did not prepare for this."

"Yeah, too fucking bad for you," I told him.

Now that I had a moment, I took a good long look at Tian Kham. He was smaller than me and, with a touch of gray on his temples, looked to be a few years older than I was. He was thin built and his hard ripped arms told me that he was in good shape.

He had also imperceptibly edged close to me as we had talked. The way he moved was so smooth I hadn't even noticed the two steps he'd taken toward me.

I raised the pistol and he snapped out a kick. The kick was hard and fast. I'd only seen a gun kicked out of someone's hand in an old movie and never figured it would work in reality.

It worked this time.

The pistol was knocked from my hand and bounced to the carpet.

I drew back my fist and threw a good straight hard right cross. It would have knocked his teeth out if that punch had landed. The problem was it didn't.

Tian Kham slapped my fist to the side as it traveled toward his face, redirecting the force past him. When my fist was past his head he grabbed my wrist, twisted it, then tossed me through the air using my own forward momentum. I hit the carpet on my back, did a roll-out and came back up to my feet.

Taking a step toward Tian Kham I saw that he was between me and the pistol. He must have known where the gun was too, but there was no way he was going to turn his back on me to go for it.

If Tan Kham had turned his back on me I'd have kicked him so hard in the ass he would have been wearing his anus for a collar and his balls for a necktie. As it was, Tian Kham just assumed a casual looking fighting stance and waited for me to come at him.

I recognized the stance and now understood that reason why he'd been able to throw me so easily. Tian Kham was a master of Aikido.

Aikido is a martial art that depends on small joint manipulation and throws. The bastard had already thrown me once like I was his personal rag doll. I couldn't afford to let him get a good hold on my fingers or my wrists or elbows. If I did, Tian Kham was likely to twist any of those joints out of their sockets.

I came at Tian Kham hard snapping out a front kick then threw a straight right followed by a left hook.

He threw me again, and when I landed this time I came down on something hard lying on the carpet.

Tian Kham realized his mistake instantly, and as I rolled and grabbed the pistol he ran and jumped at me to come down with a killing stomp.

The stomp never landed. Tian Kham was still in the air when I fired blindly up at him. The cry that Tian Kham made as the bullet hit him was something like a wounded bird would make. Tian Kham crashed to the carpet beside me and whimpered.

I rolled away and stood up over him. I didn't have any fear that Tian Kham would be kicking up at me. He wouldn't be kicking anybody ever again.

My blind shot had hit him right in the crotch.

I told him, "It's too bad I don't have the time to enjoy watching you die like this, but I got things to do."

I put a bullet through his head.

CHAPTER 49

When I stuck my head back out in the hallway everything was quiet. I waited for a few seconds to see if anyone was going to open a door or raise an alarm.

No one did.

I stepped out of the room and walked down to the door at the end of the hall that I'd entered through, and eased it open.

The two guards were gone.

After sticking my head out and taking a look around, I went outside.

It was dark out and the lights of the compound were coming on.

The moon was up and could be seen through the opening of the foliage roof directly over where the helicopter sat.

I knew I had to get moving pretty damned fast. With evening in full bloom these freaks would want to start their partying soon. Since we were supposed to be the entertainment for their celebrations it could be any moment that they'd be coming for us.

I ran back over to the building where the slaves were held and flattened myself against the wall. I was back where I had started from.

After edging over to where the corner of the building was, I decided that this was no good. Anyone seeing me from a distance standing like I was would know something was wrong. So I strolled as nonchalantly as I could over to a walkway and took a good survey of my surroundings.

I was about thirty yards from where the helicopter sat. Only open grass separated me from it.

It was quiet out here, very quiet.

I could see the front of the guest hotel. No one was coming or going out of the front door.

I could see the front of the guard's quarters. No one seemed to be moving over there.

It was quiet. I didn't even hear the night creatures of the jungle calling to each other. It was too quiet.

That was when the night exploded.

The chopper went up in a loud whoosh and the shockwave picked me up from the ground and slammed me against the brick wall of the building.

I went down in a crumpled heap, and as the darkness threatened to fall down over my head, flaming pieces of helicopter rained down all over the place.

With stars dancing at the edge of my vision I fought my way back to full consciousness in time to see other charges go off at the fence line in several places and dark dressed figures rush through the holes the explosions made.

The men coming through the fence disbursed in all directions.

I saw three of them take up a position on the ground near the door to the guards quarters. When the guards came running out of that same door a few moments later they were cut down by machine gun fire.

I was crawling back toward the side door into the slave's quarters when two of the dark dressed attackers stopped where I was and leveled their rifles on me.

I rolled over and put my hands up, and with their black and green painted faces and the dark green camouflage fatigues I instantly recognized these guys as US Special Forces.

"You're a long way from home," I said to the pair.

One raised his rifle.

The other put a restraining hand up then reached into his breast pocket and took out a photo.

He looked at the photo then asked, "Are you Dark?"

"Yeah," I told him. "And if I'd have been any closer to that chopper when you blew it up I'd be crispy too."

That made him smile.

"Nash Graham sends his regards," the soldier said.

"Tell him I said thanks," I told him as he helped me to my feet.

"Tell him yourself," the other soldier answered. "He'll be here as soon as we finish the mop-up."

CHAPTER 50

I was escorted back into the hallway where Candi waited with a crowd that looked to have grown to about thirty kids.

The higher ranked soldier told me, "Stay here. We'll be back to get you when everything is secured."

I wanted to go with him and kill some of these assholes but the truth is, what little bit I saw in the few seconds that it took to get back inside the hallway where Candi was convinced me that I was way too old to be doing this jungle fighting stuff.

These guys were fast and efficient. I saw at least ten guards riddled with machine gun fire, and the front wall of the building they were living in blown apart, all in the space of about ten seconds.

I recognized the moves these Special Forces boys were using as they combed the compound for resistance or captives. These were the same moves I used to be able to do. But that was a long time ago. Next to these guys I was like an old man just playing soldier.

*　　*　　*

In about an hour the same two soldiers who had escorted me back to Candi and the kids came and got us. The higher ranked soldier introduced himself as Sam Otto. The other soldier said his name was Mike Murphy.

A crowd of kids, somewhere around fifty, had already been rounded up and was standing in front of the building where the rest of the kids had been locked up.

Candi took the children that had been with us over to join the others. She had taken to acting like a mother hen in the last few minutes. It was good to see that. At least looking after these kids would keep her mind off of what had happened to Ron.

The kids all still looked pretty shell-shocked. I didn't know if they would ever recover. Only time would show that.

These Special Forces guys had come well prepared. They even had a bulldozer. God knows where the hell they'd got that from. They used it to knock down the front gate. It probably would have been easier if they had just unlocked the gate and driven in but they probably just mowed the gate down because it was fun to do.

After they knocked the gate down, the Special Forces guys used the dozer to push what was left of the helicopter off to the side of its landing pad.

Right after they were done, as if on cue, we could hear the beating of another chopper's blades in the sky above the trees.

* * *

In front of the guest hotel the soldiers had about fifty men lying on their faces with their hands tied behind them.

One of them was making a lot of noise.

It was that silver haired guy who appeared to be running everything here.

He tried to get to his hands and knees and a soldier shoved him back onto his face in the grass with his boot.

"You don't know who you're messing with," the silver haired man yelled at him.

"No sir, I don't," the soldier told him. "And I don't care either. I follow orders. If you try to get up again I'll use my rifle butt on your forehead."

That kept him quiet for a while.

* * *

The helicopter, beating the air with its blades, swooped in then touched down on the pad. As soon as it landed, ten more troops jumped down and ran over to where the prisoners were.

Two other men got off the military transport chopper.

One of them was a man I didn't know. He looked to be in his early thirties and wore a dark tailor made suit and dark sunglasses. He looked like one of the agents from the movie *The Men in Black*.

The other guy, I knew him pretty well. He was a little bit outside of his jurisdiction but he was a welcome sight.

The other guy was Nash Graham.

CHAPTER 51

I went over to greet Nash and we shook hands.

I shook the other guy's hand and introduced myself.

As soon as I'd said my name the other man told me, "Over here I don't officially exist. Over here, I have no name."

"Fine by me," I told him. "No Name it is."

I asked Nash, "And what are you doing over here?"

"Getting your ass out of the fire," Nash told me. "Your friend Johnny bugged me non-stop until I told him I'd check up on you. I made some calls and found out you'd be coming here and knew they would be waiting for you."

"Who the hell could you call to find out we'd be heading here?" I asked.

He glanced at No Name and both of them smiled.

Nash said, "Officially, my sources don't exist. So you won't get any names from me."

"Fine," I told him. "Thanks for coming over to lend a hand."

"It wasn't just for you," Nash said. "This here is also about a little bit of my own pay-back."

He started walking toward the group of fifty men laid out on their faces in front of the guest hotel. Nash headed specifically for that silver haired guy who had been making all the noise.

When he was standing in front of the man, Nash told the closest soldier, "stand him up."

The soldier did just that grabbing the silver haired man under the arm-pits, picking him up, and setting him back down on his feet.

"Senator Jack Craven, I assume?" Nash said to the man.

The man never even for a moment looked surprised. He never missed a beat. "You and your flunkies are in some very serious trouble," Craven spit out at him. "How dare you come into the nation of Tehan Setar and, by unauthorized military action, shut down a business operation! How..."

Nash stopped him with a raised finger in his face. "You threatened me once already and that's why we're here. You best come up with something better than that. I know about your internet kiddy-porn operation. I know about your international snuff film business. Senator, you are the one who is fucked here."

Senator Jack Craven, like any good politician, was fast on his feet or at least fast with his words. He now said, "I have business interests all over the world. If I come out of this clean I'll make every one of you very wealthy men."

"I'm listening," Nash told him.

That was when I noticed that Candi was now standing beside me. The pistol she'd taken from the guard who'd tried to rape her was in her hand down at her side.

"How much was Ron worth?" She asked the Senator.

Craven looked at her uncomprehendingly and just said, "What?"

"Oh, that's right," Candi said. "He wasn't worth anything to you. You wouldn't remember him."

She raised her gun and shot Senator Jack Craven in the right knee.

He screamed and fell to the grass on his back.

"This is for Ron!" Candi shouted and blew the Senator's other knee to pieces. "And this is for all the children you ruined." She shot Craven in the crotch and then emptied her gun in his head.

When she was done tears were running down her face. Candi turned away from us and walked back to where the children were.

Nash Graham, No Name, and I looked down at the bullet riddled corpse that had once been a US Senator.

"Well, I guess that shoots to hell any deal we might have made with him," Nash said. "It doesn't really make any difference. Even if we would have made some money off that bastard I'd have had him killed anyway."

PART III

WELCOME BACK TO MY JUNGLE

CHAPTER 52

After the entire compound had been searched, the total number of children found was right around eighty. After Nash and No Name made some calls, two well-used school busses showed up.

Candi and I escorted the children out of the compound and took them to Sister Mary Sheridon at The St. Wisdom Orphanage. The Sister assured us that she would search for the families that these children belonged with, and that the children whose families she could not locate would stay with her.

It was a big job she had ahead of her but she thanked us for bringing the children to her.

We thanked her for being there to take the kids in.

* * *

As for all of the vacationing perverts who had paid top dollar for the privilege of raping children; No Name informed us that every one of these idiots had actually been videotaped having sex with children. They would be delivered to their home country's authorities along with the evidence of their crimes.

Most, if not all of them, would soon be serving long jail sentences.

* * *

We arranged for Ron's body to be flown back to St. Louis, and three days later he had his funeral. He was buried at The Pine Bluff Cemetery next to Sherry, Lisa Rios and Kira Brooks. Pretty soon they would probably rename this place the John Dark Memorial Cemetery. If you become one of my lovers or one of my friends you may as well reserve a spot here, because this is probably where you'll be heading to before long.

*   *   *

At Ron's burial, Johnny surprised me by taking Candi in his arms and holding her as she sobbed on his shoulder. He comforted her as well as he could, and when Candi turned away from him as Ron's casket was lowered in the ground, I saw tears in Johnny's eyes.

Maybe there was hope for Johnny yet. I know that I've learned that you can never place a label on someone and expect them to be what the label says they are. Ron and Candi: one of them was a macho gay guy, the other one is a gender-blending transsexual. Both of them are two of the most brave and honorable people I've ever met.

They fit no label or stereotype, then again, nobody does.

As for me, I know I've changed. I got the revenge that I sought and it felt hollow. There was no satisfaction there. In shedding the blood of Tian Kham I found no enlightenment. There was only the empty spot in my life that Sherry used to occupy.

I have no idea what it will take to fill that void.

*   *   *

I sat in Johnny's Bar and Grill and looked out at the seven people occupying tables, downing alcohol and getting wasted in the dim light of the bar room.

Johnny poured me a Miller High Life.

I tasted it and held it up to him. "What's up?" I asked. "Normally you throw me your worst rot gut."

"Well, after what you've been through you deserve the good stuff for at least one night," he answered.

"Thanks," I said, as we clinked our glasses and then downed our beers in one drink.

He poured me another and held his glass up.

"Let's have a toast," Johnny said, "To Ron."

"And to Sherry," I added.

We clinked our glasses together again.

"We'll remember you," he said, and lifted his glass to the air.

"One other thing," I told Johnny. "After what I've seen lately, if I see someone mistreating a kid they best give their heart to god…"

"Because the rest belongs to us," Johnny finished.

"And we ain't the forgiving kind," I told him.

"You got that right," Johnny said and we slapped palms over the bar.

AFTERWORD

If only life were as simple as fiction.

The events which took place in this book are entirely fictional.

The nations of Tehan Setar as well as the child sex resort The Flesh Pit are creations of the author's imagination.

Unfortunately, the problem of women and children being sold or kidnapped for sex slaves is a reality.

Literally thousands of women and children are sold into slavery every year to be used in prostitution rings and child pornography.

In a time when The U.S. Government is using our military to police the world no one seems to want to defend the children who are being abused every day.

There are organizations which I am not at liberty to name that fight the sexual exploitation of women and children.

Please support these organizations.

Please help to end these atrocities in any way that you can.

Sincerely,
B.L. Morgan